JUNE WHATLEY

The Fine~Butterfly Detective Agency

By June Whatley

Copyright © 2021 by June Whatley

Published by Gordian Books, an imprint of Winged Publications

This book is a work of fiction. Names, characters, places, and incidents are the product of the author's imagination and are used fictitiously. Any resemblance to actual events, locales, or persons, living or dead, is coincidental.

All rights reserved including the right to reproduce this book or portions thereof in any form whatsoever – except short passages for reviews – without express permission.

ISBN: 979-8-8690-4976-6

Acknowledgements

Beta Readers read rough drafts and give feedback on the story, plot and characters.
Their input is extremely valuable.

I want to thank the Beta Readers for this book,
The Fine~Butterfly Detective Agency.
My friend, Kay W. of Northport, AL
My friend, Beverly B. of Deland, FL

And thanks to my friend Robin P. of Tuscaloosa, AL, for the idea of adding the butterfly to the sign on the cover.

Couldn't have done it without you, ladies!

Chapter 1

The Flood

Water gushed from the kitchen faucet like the fountain outside Caesar's Palace, but when it hit the ceiling, it spattered in all directions.

A hammer flew from Abigail's hand, over her shoulder, *ker-sploosh* and it clonked onto the pile of tools behind her. "I sure wish Henry was here. He was always good at this sort of mechanical stuff."

Mildred placed her hand on her sister's arm. "I know dearie, but one can't expect their hubby to last forever, now can they?"

"Stop it, Millie, don't patronize me. I know very well that a husband can't last forever, but after forty-five years of marriage, you'd think he would've at least had enough life insurance to provide for my needs."

Cocking her head, Millie replied, "Sweetie, you have enough money to last you a lifetime," she scrunched her lips, then snarled, "but you're just too stingy to pay a plumber with it."

As she zipped around to face her sister, Abigail's feet spun with a splash. "That was mean, Millie. Take it back!"

Mildred stared her straight in the eyes. "I will, when the floodwaters in this kitchen recede enough that I won't drown when I get down on my knees to beg your forgiveness."

Stomping again with a flourish, Abigail shouted, "Oh, all right then! Hand me the phone directory."

Mildred grinned and softened her tone. "With pleasure." She reached in a drawer, produced the book and handed it to her sister.

Abigail turned a few pages, then read aloud. "Ace Plumbing, how does that sound, Millie?"

"More like a detective agency, keep reading."

She perched her glasses on the end of her nose. "Okay, how about Best Plumbing?"

Mildred's forehead wrinkled. "Hmmm, no, too smug."

Abigail flung the thin, small-town phonebook at her sister. "Okay, then you decide."

Mildred caught the book and out of habit, she licked her fingers even though they dripped with water, she turned to the correct page, adjusted her glasses and scanned the listings. "Ah, here we go, Cranky Pants Plumbing."

Her sister rolled her eyes, then blew out air in an exasperated fashion. "You've got to be kidding me."

Mildred looked over the top of her glasses. "Nope, this is our man. He's not trying to impress us and since he's old enough to be a *Cranky Pants*, then he must have experience. Yes, this is the man for us, I can feel it in my bones. Hand me your cellphone."

Abigail reached in her pocket and pulled out her phone.

Numbers chirped in, "I'm amazed it still works."

It rang several times before a man answered. "Hello."

Mildred replied, "Hello, is this Mr. Cranky Pants?"

Even Abigail could hear the laughter. "Why yes, it is, sugar. How can I hep ya?"

"My sister and I either need a plumber or an ark, can you provide either of those services?"

Through the receiver, they both heard the man laugh again. "Sounds like a big job. Do you know where the water cut-off valve is outside your house?"

Mildred nodded, but only Abigail saw. "Yes, we do," then shook her head, "but we can't seem to locate the do-lolly that you use to turn it with."

"Okay, I see on the Caller ID that you're with the Fine~Butterfly Detective Agency, what's the address? I'll come right over."

A thumbs up flashed toward Abigail. "We're located at the corner of Hines and Fentress. You can't miss us, there's water running from the house, into the street."

Within a few minutes, a clunky, faded-brown truck pulled up to the curb in front of their house, a skinny fellow in bib overalls jumped out carrying a long, straight bar with a t-shaped handle at one end and a forky-thing at the other.

The girls leaned to the window and stared out while the water spurted to the ceiling between them, cascading down over their already drenched bodies.

Just beneath the detective agency sign, the elderly gent opened a metal cover in the ground and bent to close the valve, the sign bonked him in the head as he worked. The squeak of the rusty valve could be heard all the way in the house, as the amount of water surging from the faucet diminished to a trickle.

"Whew," Mildred wiped her forehead, "I think we're rescued."

"Well, that's wonderful for you, but look at this place. I can already see the planks of my dining room floor starting to curl on the edges. This will take a week to clean up."

Ding-dong!

Placing both hands on her sister's back, she nudged her forward. "Don't keep the man waiting, Abby. Time is money; let's see how much that pitchfork-thing cost you?"

When Abigail managed to pull the door open, a torrent of water rushed out, creating whitewater rapids down the stone steps.

Mildred scooted to her sister's side and propelled her hand forward. "Hello, I'm Mildred Butterfly and this is my sister Abigail Fine, you must be Mr. Cranky Pants."

Bahahaha, the man bent double and slapped his leg. "I like you lady. You can call me Cranky, or you can call me George, take your pick."

Without any hesitation, she replied, "Well, Cranky, my sister and I are in your debt."

"You're darn tootin' you are, darlin.' The call-out fee on the weekend is two hundred dollars, but I turned the curb key for free," he winked, "just as a courtesy, you see." He snickered and pushed his way in. "I need to see what's goin' on in there." He slogged his rubber boots past the women and followed the stream of water racing from the kitchen.

An array of tools lay sprawled on the floor. The kitchen table had a bird cage on top, the door was open, but with no bird in sight. "What in tarnation went on in here?"

Mildred waded in behind him. "You see, Cranky, my sister's husband passed away and left his beloved parrot in her care. She had asked me to move in with her when Henry passed, Henry was her husband, not the parrot. Anyway, I myself, also being widowed, decided to move in, but that darn bird took an instant dislike to me. I'm not sure why, maybe it's the smell of the shampoo I use or … sorry, I digress. So, this afternoon, I came into the kitchen to make a cup of tea and when I bent over to see if the flame had ignited, my fanny accidentally pushed against the cage and that stupid culprit bit me."

George bahaha-ed again. "And how does that lead to a broken faucet and all this mess?"

"Well, Cranky, you see, I had my right hand on the handle of the teapot and when that *Pirate's Pal* bit my booty, I shot up like an arrow, my arms flew back and all I know is the kettle, full of water, hit the faucet, my backside knocked over the birdcage and all heck broke loose in here. Abigail heard the bird squawking, came running in, slipped and fell, she saw the birdcage in the water and yanked it up, the door sprang open, that ridiculous parrot rocketed to the ceiling and clung to the light fixture. I climbed on a chair and tried to grab him, but the chair wobbled and I twirled around like a whirly dervish, toppled and landed in the sink, that must be when the bottle brush got jammed into the garbage disposal and when I reached back to try to push myself out of the basin, my hand hit the disposal switch. It made an awful racket for a couple of seconds, then stopped. Water started to rise in the sink, so Abby figured it was clogged. She opened the closet door to get the Plumber's Helper and when she pulled it out, the lip of the plunger hooked on the edge of the ironing board. Well, down it came with quite a clatter, I tell you—barely missing poor Abby's head."

He he he! "Go on, sugar, I'm luvin' this."

"Well, as I said," placing her fingers beside her mouth, "all *heck* broke out in here. Then Abigail looked for that forky-thing to go outside and turn off the water, but the flood was getting deep and she was afraid to open the basement door for fear of unleashing a Pandora's Box down there. All she could find up here, besides the plunger and ironing board, of course, was a wrench, a screwdriver, a saw, a fly swatter and a hammer. That's when my cool head took charge and called you, Mr. Cranky Pants."

"Well, gals, I can tell ya, that's the best dang story I've heard since before my Shelly passed away. It's been nearly three years and I needed some entertainment tonight."

Abigail flung her head back, hoisting her chin into the air. "I'm glad that someone finds this funny! As for me, I'm just sick at the thought of how we'll manage here for a week while this place gets cleaned up."

George wheeled toward her. "A week? No way, sugar, you're looking at a month's worth of work here."

Mildred leaned forward. "A month? How are we going to live here for a month with no kitchen?"

"Well, that's simple darlin,' you ain't."

Her eyebrows drew together. "Ain't what?"

George laughed. "You ain't gonna live here while this place is being worked on. There'll be ripping out, sawing, sawdust, spraying anti-fungal solution, hammering and all sorts of dangerous stuff. Heaven forbid they find some asbestos, this house is kinda old you know, that'd take a whole special crew."

Abigail threw her hands to her cheeks. "How much is this going to cost?"

Mildred declared, "And how are we going to eat?"

George stepped between the wide-eyed sisters and placed a hand on each of their shoulders. "Don't worry now, gals, I'll call my grandson and see if he can come over for a quick look-see. He's a good lad and does good work."

Abigail blinked. "A good lad, how old is your grandson?"

"Oh, don't worry now, sugar, he's mid-twenties and fit as a fiddle. He's got a fine crew and they'll set'er right in here in no time."

George left the house and went to his truck.

Abigail glared through the kitchen window. "Millie, how am I going to pay for this?"

"Don't be ridiculous, Abby. You have house insurance, it should cover this just fine. We can stay at a hotel until the work is finished."

"But … "

"Stop it, Abby, here comes Cranky Pants." She

glanced toward her sister. "And close your mouth, dear, before the parrot poops in it. By the way," she scanned the room, "where is that despicable bird?"

George entered the kitchen rubbing his hands together. "Ladies, you're in luck. My grandson finished a job yesterday and can start work Monday. He'll be here in a jiffy to look the place over and start working up an estimate."

Abigail faced him. "But … "

"Now don't you worry, Ms. Abigail. He's a good boy, he'll treat you right and look," he pointed to the kitchen floor, "the water's just about gone already, of course, we don't know where it's all gone too yet." He grinned.

Abigail's eyes fluttered. "Is the room spinning?"

Several minutes later, Abigail awoke on the sofa in the living room. She lifted the back of her hand to her forehead. "What … what happened?"

Mildred sat on the edge next to her and patted her free hand. "You fainted, dearest. Cranky Pants caught you, but you were as limp as a wet noodle, so he couldn't carry you. Luckily his grandson came in about that time and lifted you like you were a dried prune and carried you to the couch."

"I fainted?" She sat up and her eyebrows knit together. "What do you mean like a dried prune?"

Mildred laughed. "Oh, don't get your knickers in a knot. Turn around here and meet Tony."

A very handsome young man approached and extend his hand. "Hello, ma'am, I'm Anthony. George is my gramps. Are you feeling better?"

Abigail tilted her head back to take in the whole scope of his frame, a light from behind his head threw a glow like a halo all around him. All that was lacking was the sound of a choir of angels singing. She smiled. "Yes, I believe I'm feeling better. Thank you for coming to my rescue, Anthony."

George cackled. "Okay, girls, enough moony-eyeing of my grandson. He has that effect on women, now let the boy get to work."

Anthony pointed. "What's back there?"

Abigail glanced over her shoulder. "That's the office, dear."

"Do you mind if I start in there and work my way to the kitchen?"

"That will be fine, Anthony, whatever you need to do."

Several doors opened then shut, light switches flicked on and off, then a door in the hallway creaked open.

"Uh-oh, we've got a problem down here. I'll run to the shop to get my sup-pump and get it started tonight, that is, if you ladies are willing to hire me."

Abigail pushed her feet off the sofa, stood and drifted toward the basement door with her hand in the air. "Oh, yes, Anthony, you must start work as soon as possible."

Mildred glanced over at George and rolled her eyes.

George covered his mouth to stifle the *hee hee hee,* so Abigail wouldn't hear, then he whispered to Mildred, "I told you he was a good lad," then he winked.

Anthony entered the room and rubbed his hands together. "All-righty-then, I'll be off and back straight away, in the meantime, you ladies try to locate the infamous parrot. I'll have to turn the power off after I set the pump to run on a generator, that way we can prevent any further unfortunate mishaps." He dashed out the front door, down the steps and to his truck.

Abigail and Mildred watched him as he sprinted across the lawn and hopped behind the steering wheel.

Abigail reminisced aloud. "Do you remember when Henry and Max could run like that?"

Mildred tipped her head to the side, pursed her lips and frowned. "Actually, no, my Max could never do more than a heavy jog."

"Oh, Millie!"

"What? It's true. Henry was the athletic one, Max was his lumbering best friend. Come on Abby, let's find that darn booty-biter."

Abigail snarled. "Why don't you just stick out your bum again? I'm sure he'll find us."

George laughed. "Come on now, gals, it's been an emotional evening. Let's stop sniping."

"Of course, you're right, Mr. Cranky Pants. Come on Abby, let me help you find that darn parrot."

Chapter 2

A Pleasant Surprise

A butterfly net, given to Mildred as a joke by her husband when they first married, aided in the capture of the ornery parrot. Now with the occupied birdcage in-hand, Abigail and Mildred surveyed the damage in the kitchen.

George leaned against the counter. He and Anthony glanced toward Abigail and Mildred, then George gave his grandson a nod.

Anthony grinned. "Ladies, I have a surprise for you."

Abigail smiled. "What kind of a surprise, dear?"

"While I was inspecting the house, I noticed your

Homeowners' Insurance Policy lying on the desk in the study. I've worked with your company before, so I made a call."

Abigail smiled. "And what did they say, Anthony?"

"I asked my friend Simone to do a quick check of your coverage. She said that your hotel, food, transportation, all expenses will be covered by their company while you are displaced due to repairs."

Abigail's eyes were fixed on him. "That's nice, dear."

"My friend Simone went on to say you could either check into a luxury hotel for a month, or and here's the surprise, you can go on a month-long cruise to the Caribbean. How does that sound?"

Mildred stepped forward. "What? You've got to be kidding? Even if that were true, how could we get booked on a cruise at such short notice?"

George leaned back and laughed. "Here's the kicker, girls. Go ahead, Tony, wow the ladies."

"Simone's sister is a travel agent and had just told her that she has a luxury suite that was canceled at the last minute. The people forfeited a large deposit and the insurance company can save that much money on your fare. So, what do you say, ladies? Do I escort you to the Grand Palace Hotel tonight or to the Princess of the Sea, which leaves for the Caribbean in the morning?"

Cranky Pants leaned in. "So, what will it be, gals? Tropical breezes, pristine Caribbean blue water, gorgeous sandy beaches? Or the familiar view of your city? Either way, you girls need to go pack, think about it, will it be: swimsuits, sunhats and suntan lotion; or city duds?" He chuckled. "Now don't take too long to decide, you need to be out of here in a couple of hours, so we can shut the electricity off."

An hour or so later, their suitcases clacked against the rails, as they descended the stairs into the living room.

With his hands in his pockets, George rocked back and forth from heel to toe and asked, "Well, girlies, what did you pack?"

Abigail turned to Anthony. "Just how far is it to the pier, dear?" Then shifting her eyes from Anthony to George, she picked up the birdcage and pushed it forward. "And which one of you is going to take care of Black Beard while we're gone?"

George reached for the cage. "Don't forget your passports, girls," and he laughed.

They scurried to the office. "Where did we put those, Millie?"

The carpet squished beneath their feet.

Mildred announced, "Here they are, let's get out of this swamp."

Chapter 3

Remorse

At a speed less comfortable than Mildred would have preferred, Anthony raced toward the dock.

Abigail chattered away. "My, you're such a good driver, Anthony and you seem so familiar with this area."

"Yes, ma'am, my family does a lot of work down here."

Mildred leaned forward to look past her sister, so she could see the side of Anthony's face. "Really, what kind of work, Tony? Does your granddad do plumbing-work down here."

He nodded. "You might say that, they need him on the ship from time to time." The brakes screeched. "Here we are, Ms. Abigail, Ms. Mildred, I'll get your luggage checked in."

A lone porter waited at the foot of the gangway, his elbow propped on the handle of a luggage carrier.

Anthony wrestled all of their bags onto the flat, hand-truck and turned to Abigail and Mildred. "This man will take your bags to your room while we check you two in on deck." He looked at the porter. "Take these to the Princess Suite, please," and he handed the man some money.

Abigail moaned. "Oh, Anthony, I should've taken care of that, I'm still not thinking straight. I'm so sorry."

He took her hand and smiled. "That's not a problem, Ms. Abigail, your insurance company will reimburse me. Come this way, please."

"You're such a delightful boy, Anthony."

He led them up the stairs of the gangway, at the top, stood a waiting crew member. Anthony addressed the officer. "This is Ms. Abigail Fine and Ms. Mildred Butterfly, I believe Simone called to arrange everything."

"Yes, sir, Mr. Anthony, we've prepared their

stateroom and we'll take very good care of them."

Anthony turned to Abigail. "This gentleman will take you to your cabin and I'll text you updates on your house repairs. I even took the liberty of having Simone updating your phone plan to include International calls, so you won't be charged extra for texts back and forth, or when we talk while you're on the cruise."

Abigail flinched. "You did what?"

"Don't worry, it will revert back to your regular plan at the end of the month and it will save you a bundle on your next phone bill. Also, ladies, I've been ordered by my Gramps to tell you, you are not to worry about your house and you are to have a very good time. When you return, all of the work will be finished and you'll have a lovely, like-new home."

"Anthony dear, *do* be careful and *do* try to stay within the budget."

His grin put her mind at ease. "Yes, ma'am and *you* try to relax."

As Anthony bounded down the stairs, the officer motioned for another crewman to come take his place as guard at the stairway, then said, "This way ladies," he pointed across the deck with his open palm. "I'll show you to your cabin. It is, by the way, the nicest one on the ship."

Abigail looked at Mildred. "Oh my, this sounds fancy."

When they arrived at the room, the officer swiped a plastic card across a keypad, turned the handle and the door swung inward. "Ladies," and again, his open palm pointed the way. As they stepped across the threshold, plush carpet the color of Sand, embraced their feet. He handed the key to Mildred. "Please enjoy your cruise, ladies." He backed away, closing the door behind him.

Inside their luxurious cabin, they soaked-in the beauty of the room. At the head of the king-sized bed, small crystal chandeliers hung above each side table, a tone-on-tone floral cream-colored duvet flowed glamorously to the floor. To their left was the bathroom, glistening with chrome and white enamel, to the right of the entryway was a large closet made of light-colored teak wood and a matching dresser with three drawers on each end, connected by a small work surface, a mirror hung overhead and a teak stool adorned with a little cream-colored cushion, sat in the middle.

Mildred walked to the far side where drapes matching the bedspread hung. They were slightly parted and she pushed them aside enough to reveal a sliding glass door with a balcony and deck furniture outside. "Abigail look! This is heavenly."

Standing, in the midst of their luggage, her sister flailed her arms, Mildred turned toward her. "Oh, Millie, what were we thinking? We are leaving our home in the hands of complete strangers." Then her voice came out deeper than normal as she leaned toward her sister. "Come to think of it, Millie, I don't remember having our insurance policy out on the desk in the office. And the nerve of Simone changing my phone plan without asking me. Another thing, did you hear that man at the entryway call him, Mr. Anthony, without even being introduced? Something is fishy about all of this."

"Abigail, his name was printed on his uniform shirt, didn't you notice?" Stepping toward her sister, Mildred took her elbow and guided her to the bed. "Sit down, dear, it's been a stressful day and we should've prayed about this, but with all of the confusion … we didn't.

Besides it doesn't matter how we got here, it's too late to change the plan now, so let's pray." Mildred tenderly held her sister's hand and they bowed their heads. "Father, we come to you and ask for forgiveness for being such foolish, gullible women and we ask you to take charge of this mess. Please protect our home and my sister's resources, confuse any plan of the enemy that is set against us, Lord. In the name of Jesus. Amen." Mildred opened her eyes and patted Abigail's arm. "Now dear, the best thing we can do is to get some sleep, I'm sure things will look better in the morning."

Chapter 4

The Next Day

Just about eight, they awoke to the sound of feet, scrambling outside their stateroom.

Abigail stretched and yawned. "I wonder what all of the commotion's about?"

Mildred reached for her robe and poked her arms into the sleeves. "Let me take a quick peek." She crossed the sides of her robe in front, tied the belt and cracked the door just enough to see numerous porters shuffling bags into various cabins.

One porter abruptly turned and ended up facing her, his eyes flew open wide. "Oh, pardon me, ma'am. I didn't know any passengers had come aboard yet."

"That's quite alright, young man, we were allowed

to board last night."

As Mildred backed clear of the door the man said, "That is highly unusual, you must be a very special guest. If you need anything, anything at all, please call me. My name's Isaac."

"Thank you, Isaac. I'll keep that in mind." She closed the door and leaned against it. "You know, Abby, this might not be so bad. We've already asked forgiveness for being so naive and asked for protection of the house and your finances. We also asked God to protect us against any plans of the enemy, so I'm thinking we've got this covered." She smiled. "What do you say, we get dressed and find some coffee? This could be fun."

Abigail groaned, but agreed. "Alright! I could use some breakfast too. In all of the chaos last night, we didn't get any dinner."

Mildred patted her tummy. "You know, I thought I felt a growl down there." She smiled at her sister and reached for a suitcase. "I don't need a shower this morning, Caesar's fountain took care of that last night." She laughed and tossed a fresh outfit onto the bed. "And my hair dried naturally, so I'll just sport my curls today."

Abigail shuffled to the bathroom and turned on the water. "I'll only be a minute. Would you pick an outfit for me too? Just not too matchy-matchy, like Mom used to do."

Her sister laughed. "Roger wilco."

In about half an hour, they emerged from their stateroom.

Mildred wore a pair of turquoise, capris with a white T-shirt, on the front of the blouse was a picture of a basket filled with peach-colored flowers, clear crystal beads glittered in the center of each blossom. A sunhat with a turquoise band, also embellished with clear crystals, leaned causally against the basket, as if it had been tossed there by its former wearer.

Abigail had on white capris with a turquoise T-shirt. The picture on the front of her top was a pile of seashells scattered next to a sandcastle, crystal beads glittered in the sand. "I asked you not to go matchy-matchy, Millie."

"I didn't, dear. Your shirt has shells and a castle, mine has a hat and a basket of flowers."

"Oh, Millie, your turquoise on the bottom, I'm

turquoise on the top."

Mildred smiled. "Exactly, dear." In the corridor, she spotted the porter. "Oh Isaac, which way should two very caffeine-deprived ladies go to find the refueling station?"

Isaac's eyebrows rose. "Excuse me, ma'am?"

Abigail poked her sister in the side with her elbow. "She mean's where's the coffee, dear."

He smiled, stepped to the side and gestured. "Down this hallway, through the double doors, in the breezeway go to the left and the dining room will be on your right. Have a wonderful day, ladies." He nodded and continued rolling luggage through the passageway.

The corners of Abigail's mouth turned south. "I wonder if we should have tipped him?"

"Don't be ridiculous, Abby. He just gave you directions, he didn't carry you there." She spun the way Isaac had indicated. "Come on, don't dawdle. I need coffee."

Only seconds later they opened the dining room door.

Mildred froze. "Abby, we're the only people in here.

Where is everybody?

From behind, a warm, friendly voice greeted them. "Good morning, ladies."

They turned, face-to-face, with a tall, handsome man of about fifty, wearing a dazzling white uniform. "I'm Captain Jeremiah Williams, at your service and to answer your question, the other passengers are boarding now." He spread his hands to pan the room. "Within a couple of hours this place will be teeming with guests."

Mildred thrust her hand toward him. "Captain Williams, it's a pleasure to meet you, I'm Mildred Butterfly and this," she glanced to her side, "this is my sister Abigail Fine."

He grasped her hand and glanced toward Abigail. "Ladies, please feel free to call me, Jeremiah," he leaned forward, "or I will have to insist that you call me, Captain Baby." He whispered, "And I have a message for you from a gentleman," he cleared his throat, "named Cranky Pants, who wishes me to tell you that everything is under control at the house," his eyebrows drew close together and a questioning tone slipped out, "even Black Beard is fine and you're to have a wonderful time."

Mildred laughed as she withdrew her hand. "You mean Cranky Pants actually called you?"

"Well, the message was passed to me, but I assure you, by all accounts, his wishes were heart-felt."

Mildred turned to her sister and laughed. "See Abby, everything is going to be fine," she looked back, "Now which way to the coffee pot, Captain Baby?"

With a warm, fun-loving laugh, the Captain motioned. "Allow me to accompany you." He strode past row after row of pastries and at the very end a gigantic coffee urn stood steaming.

The delightful aroma greeted their nostrils.

Abigail folded her hands under her chin and pushed her shoulders toward her ears. "Oh, my that nutty smell is wonderful."

"That's the Arabica and Hazelnut blend that we import especially for our cruises." The Captain held a small teacup beneath the spout, twisted the handle and filled it to an appropriate level, then offered it to Abigail. "Please try some."

With a deep inhale, she sampled the aroma, then lifted the porcelain vessel to her lips. A quiet sip produced a long sigh. "Oh, my. That's delicious." And she pushed the cup to Mildred, "Want a taste?"

"No, thank you, I'll have a large cup, if you please," she looked at him, raised one eyebrow and grinned, "Captain Baby."i

With a roar of laughter, he reached for a fresh cup. "I can see that I'm going to have to keep my eye on you two." He filled the mug and handed it to Mildred, then topped off Abigail's. "Since you have been here overnight, you might like something more satisfying than pastries. May I point out," he gestured to the far side of the room, "that a small steamtable is available with eggs, pancakes, sausage and a variety of other more substantial offerings, over there, under the window on the starboard side of the room."

Abigail pointed. "Look, sister," and a long moan of the word, "foooood," slipped out.

The Captain tipped his head. "Enjoy, ladies."

It didn't take long for Mildred and Abigail to avail themselves of at least one serving of every delectable item on the table.

Leaning back, Mildred stuck her thumbs in her waistband and sighed. "Oh, my goodness, I wish I had brought more pants with elastic at the waist. I may have to shop for clothes before we leave the harbor."

"Nonsense, Millie, as soon as you stand up, it'll all drop to that big pouch that hangs below your waist."

"Abigail! Honestly! You can be so curt. I can't help it if I got our father's bone structure, and I can hardly believe we were brought up by the same mother."

"Oh, don't get your panties in a twist. I'm sorry. Don't be angry with me, Millie," she smiled, "let's go exploring."

They exited the room through the opposite door from where they had entered. Fresh sea air rushed across their faces. Mildred strolled to the rail. "Abby, look at all of those people down there."

Abigail tiptoed and leaned forward. "They look like ants! How high up do you think we are?"

Mildred leaned to view the ship's exterior. "I don't know, it feels like fifteen stories, but I doubt that it's more than ten."

Abigail leaned back and placed her hand on her

forehead. "Let's go explore somewhere else, even with only ten stories my head is spinning."

Mildred moved away from the rail and groaned. "Oh, this is going to be a fun cruise, I can see it now." Then she pointed to a schematic on the wall. "Look, we can do some exploring from this spot," and placed her hand on the drawing. "It looks like there are ten decks for passengers and more below that for the crew and mechanical operations."

Abigail placed her hand on her stomach. "Swell!"

"Look, Abby, this is where we are and our suite is in this passageway. At least we're close to the top if we need to get out in a hurry."

Eyes darted toward her sister. "What do you mean, Millie, in case we need to get out in a hurry."

Mildred's eyes never moved from the ship plans, but a slight gleam lit them. "Nothing, dear, nothing at all."

Abigail placed her finger on the map and shot back. "Oh, and look, there's the gym, you won't need to go buy new clothes after all."

A buttery voice sliced through the tension. "Good morning, ladies, can either of you point me in the direction of the dining hall?"

They both turned to examine the owner of the new voice.

Mildred eyed the man head-to-toe and spoke first. "As you can see by this drawing, we are here." She turned her gaze to the wall and touched the diagram, "and," she lifted her arm to point, "that door ten paces away, that's the dining hall."

The smile melted from Abigail's face. "Millie!"

The man removed his Panama hat with a narrow, green band and tipped his head. His lean, straight nose pointed to a thin mustache resting on his upper lip, above a gleaming white smile. "Thank you and allow me to introduce myself, I am Ferdinand Modesto."

Abigail offered her hand. "Hello, I'm Abigail Fine and this," she glanced at her sister, "is my older sister, Mildred Butterfly."

"Thank you for the directions, ladies, it would be my great honor if you would joined me for some breakfast, if you have not yet dined." He took Abigail's hand and rather than shaking it, he lifted her tiny knuckles to his lips and gave them a light kiss.

Her eyelashes fluttered. "Yes, thank you, Mr. Modesto. It would be our pleasure to join you … "

Her sister interrupted. "But we've just finished our breakfast and were about to go exploring. Perhaps another time."

He tipped his head forward and replaced his hat. "Thank you, ladies."

As he stepped toward the dining room, Abigail swatted Mildred's wrist. "Why did you do that?"

Squinched brows and pursed lips bore down on Abigail. "Are you out of your mind? Because that guy is as greasy as an eel. Your hand should feel like an oil slick."

"Oh, nonsense, Millie, he was just being friendly. You were rude."

Mildred's head tilted to the side. "And you're never rude, are you, Abby?"

Her fists tightened and punched toward the deck. "Okay, Millie, let's stop this. I'm sorry I was rude about your tummy pouch and I'll try to be a little more adventurous."

A smile greeted Abigail. "And I shall try to be more

polite to oily, queasy, passengers who are trying to be friendly. Is it a deal?"

"Oh, do be serious, Millie. Let's make our way back to our room and hang up our clothes."

Mildred hooked her arm in her sister's. "Okay, come on, Abby. We never fought like this when our husbands were alive."

Abigail frowned as they walked. "We rarely saw each other when they were alive, now that we live together, it's like our teenage years all over again."

Mildred smiled. "Except without pimples, dear. Now let's cut through here, the boat seems to be pushing away from the pier."

Chapter 5

A Visitor

In their stateroom, Abigail busied herself removing clothes from a suitcase. "Which side of the closet would you like, Millie, I'll give you first choice."

"It doesn't really matter as long as I get to keep the side of the bed closest to the bathroom. Those nighttime trips are annoying, especially if I have to go all the way around the bed."

"Okay, if you get the side of the bed toward the bathroom, I'll give you the half of the closet on the bathroom side of the room."

"That works for me," Mildred smiled.

Three light taps on the door drew Abigail's attention.

She stepped over, turned the handle, and was greeted with a great surprise. "Why, Mr. Modesto, what are you doing here?"

Mildred leaned away from her suitcase to view the man.

"Please, madam, call me Ferdinand. I took the liberty of asking the porter which room was occupied by the two charming ladies. He immediately knew of whom I spoke and please, allow me to apologize for the awkwardness of our earlier meeting. I am traveling alone and I saw two," he leaned to peer toward Mildred, "very attractive ladies and I wished to make their acquaintance. Would you both do me the honor of joining me for luncheon today?"

Abigail smiled, then looked back at her sister. "We have no prior engagement for lunch."

Mildred cleared her throat.

Abigail turned to Ferdinand again. "Though my sister seems to be coming down with a cold and may not be able to join us."

Mildred thrust her head back with her eyes toward the ceiling. "No, I'm fine, we would be happy to join you, Ferdinand."

He smiled. "Shall I call for you at twelve and escort you to the dining room?"

Abigail beamed. "That would be wonderful." As she slid the door closed, she tilted her head to retain eye contact with him until the very last second.

Mildred groaned. "Good grief, Abby, talk about our teenage years. That was revolting."

"Oh, stop it, Grumpy Britches. Henry's been gone for more than three years and it's nice to have a man pay attention to me again."

"I know, dearie, but you're too trusting, I worry about you."

Abigail began humming a tune. "Let's finish this closet and get changed for lunch."

With a groan, her sister asked, "Changed? Why are we changing?"

"We need something more 'ship-board' and festive for our luncheon engagement, dear."

Mildred folded her arms. "I'm not changing. We just put these clothes on a couple of hours ago and I'm telling you, Abby, that guy is trouble. He's rushing us into this supposed friendship-triangle and something just isn't right about it. He's too, oh, I don't know, too faky somehow. I even thought his mustache might've been drawn on with Magic Marker. He just isn't real."

Abigail stood in front of her sister and folded her arms to match Mildred's. "Well, I think he's real and he's romantic."

"Too romantic!" snapped Mildred.

"And I think he's a gentleman."

"A hyper-supersonic-gentleman."

"And he's thoughtful." Abigail turned her back to her sister.

"Too thoughtful, dear. 'If something seems too good to be true. It probably is!'"

Abigail turned around. "Is what?"

"Oh, Abby, it's that old saying, 'If something seems too good to be true. It probably is … or should that be, it probably isn't? Anyway, dog-gone-it, it means if something seems too good to be true, it probably isn't true." Mildred's forehead furrowed. "I tell you what, Abby. Let's put him to the test."

"What do you mean by 'put him to the test,' Millie?"

"Let's join him in his game and see how real he really is."

Abigail twisted her head slightly to the side. "How are we going to do that?"

"We'll let him think everything is alright and we'll pretend to enjoy his company until he slips up."

Abigail frowned. "Slips up, how?"

"Oh Abby, for goodness sake! I'll handle everything, you just enjoy Mr. Greasy's company."

She smiled. "I think I can do that. Wonderful plan, Millie, simply wonderful."

Chapter 6

Right on Time

Promptly at noon, a *tap, tap, tap* alerted them to Ferdinand's presence.

When Abigail opened the door, his smile captivated her, but with his hat in one hand and flowers in the other, she drew her palms to her heart. "Why, Ferdinand, how thoughtful of you. The last time a gentleman gave me flowers, was the delivery boy from the florist at my husband's funeral. How totally unexpected and sweet. Thank you!"

"My pleasure, dear lady." He separated the offering of flowers. "And a bouquet for your sister too." He scanned the room behind Abigail and smiled. "Are you and she ready for a culinary adventure?"

Abigail turned to face her sister. "Millie, are you ready or should Ferdinand and I go ahead?"

Arriving at her side, "No, dearest, I'm ready. Shall we get this new venture started? Lead the way, Ferdinand."

He handed each a small nosegay, then stepping aside, offered each a bent elbow. "I shall be the most envied man on this ship," he smiled.

Their stroll to the dining room took only seconds.

On their way there, Abigail asked, "Ferdinand, is this your first trip to the Caribbean?"

"Gracious no, I travel for my work and I have been here many times. Perhaps I can show you the sights while we are in port."

Mildred continued the conversation. "That would be lovely. What type of work do you do?"

Ferdinand removed his elbow from Mildred's arm and reached for the door, a slight bow followed. "Ladies, after you and to answer your question, madam, I am in acquisitions."

It had been impossible to see through the tinted

windows, but upon entering the room, Abigail and Mildred's shoulders jerked back. Earlier in the morning they had had the gigantic room to themselves; now it clattered with plates, clanked with glasses, and swarmed with people.

Abigail leaned toward Ferdinand. "So much for a quiet, intimate lunch."

"Do not be worried, dear lady, I have reserved a table for us."

She gasped and placed her hands together. "Oh, how thoughtful of you!"

He led the way to the buffet and handed each lady a plate. "Please, help yourselves and I shall secure drinks for us. What would you like, Ms. Fine?"

"A glass of sweet tea would be delightful, thank you."

"And you, Ms. Butterfly?"

"Yes, thank you, sweet tea with a slice of lemon."

He rushed toward the beverage island.

Mildred followed Abigail to the buffet line. "I tell you, Abby, I don't trust that man."

"Relax, Millie, what can possibly happen to us here?

There are dozens of people around."

She surveyed the room. "I know, but he's just too *oily* for me."

"Oh, Millie, do relax. After all, you're the one who said we'd prayed and asked the Lord to foil the plans of the enemy."

"I know, Abby, but we are also supposed to be as wise as serpents and as gentle as doves."ii

Abigail turned to face her sister. "I have an idea," she placed her finger on her chest, "I'll play the part of the dove," she moved her finger to rest against Mildred's collar bone, "and you be the serpent." She turned back around to scoop a large dollop of Crab Delight onto her plate.

Mildred growled, "Ohhhh, Abigail, you can be so cantankerous."

Ferdinand returned with an empty plate. "Ladies, I have deposited our beverages at our table," he pointed, "just over there and may I step in here with you?"

Abigail yielded way. "Certainly, Ferdinand."

With plates filled, he guided the ladies to a wonderful

table with a view of the sea and a curved, tinted glass ceiling which displayed puffy clouds overhead.

"Oh, Ferdinand, this is a marvelous table. Thank you so much for thinking to reserve it for us." She took in the expanse of the room. "The only tables left available are in the middle."

"It was my pleasure, dear lady. I wished for you and your sister to have the best seats in the house. Such charming ladies should not be cramped into the middle of a crowd, you should survey the festivities from your thrones." He pulled out the chair for Abigail and gave a small push once she was seated.

Abigail giggled. "Oh, how sweet."

Mildred seated herself and stared at her sister with an intense scowl. "We need to eat before our food gets cold."

Ferdinand agreed. "Yes, we should savor every delectable morsel?"

Ooos and awws accompanied every mouthful and the conversation revolved around the beauty and amenities of the ship.

Finally, Ferdinand asked, "Ladies, would you like some dessert? I'll be glad to go claim any delicacy you would like."

Abigail answered, "No, my goodness, I couldn't eat another bite?"

He looked across the table at Mildred. "And you, dear lady?"

"Yes, I think I'll try some of that flaming stuff," she pointed, "over there in the middle of the dessert table."

"Excellent choice, Ms. Butterfly. That delightful dish is Baked Alaska," he stood, "I shall demand a slice for each of us."

Abigail cleared her throat. "Well, since you're going anyway, I may try," she held up her almost-touching index finger and thumb, "the tiniest little slice."

Ferdinand rose and bent in her direction. "Your wish is my command, madam."

Abigail bunched her shoulders toward her ears and smiled. "Thank you!"

As he strode away, Abigail glanced at Mildred whose face glared back. "Abby you are making me nauseous. Would you stop acting like a silly schoolgirl!"

Abigail's lips pouted out. "You're just jealous because he favors me over you."

Mildred bristled. "I am not."

"Are too."

"Am not!"

At that moment, large portions of the dramatic dessert were placed before each lady who smiled at her plate, then up at their server.

Abigail's eyes widened. "Isaac what're you doing here? Where's Ferdinand?"

"The gentleman will be only a moment, ladies. He asked me to offer an apology and to assure you he would return as quickly as possible. In the meantime, please enjoy your dessert." He turned and walked away.

Picking up a fork, each dipped out a small sample and raised it to their mouths.

"Oh, my goodness, this is divine," groaned Mildred. "I just smashed the dessert to the roof of my mouth with my tongue. You don't even have to chew, it just melts."

"I must say, this is delightful," added Abigail.

At that instant, Ferdinand arrived with a smile and his own plate piled high with dessert. "I'm glad you are pleased." He seated himself and raised a fork full of cake, chocolate crumble, ice cream and meringue. "Too large for one bite, I know, but the blend of flavors is exquisite." He loaded his mouth and moaned. "Hmmm, magnifique!"

Abigail's eyes twinkled. "Oh, you speak French?"

"But of course," he turned and smiled at her, but with cake crumbs lodged in his mustache and cooed, "it is the language of love."

Mildred raised her napkin to her lips to stifle a laugh, which came out more like a cough into the folded square of cloth.

Abigail shot her a look as she lifted her napkin. "Here, let me help you. You have a little food on your lip."

Color quickly spread up his face. "How embarrassing and you are so genteel and so enchanting."

"Think nothing of it, Ferdinand." She glared at her sister. "A man should have a good appetite."

When she withdrew her hand, he blotted his lips with his own napkin. "Let's finish our dessert and I have a surprise for you."

Abigail's fork clinked onto her plate. "What surprise? I have to know."

"I have learned that there will be a special event in the rotunda this evening and I would like for you to join me again," he paused and glanced at each, "for dinner, followed by an evening of dancing and a stroll on the deck?"

Abigail's eyes lit up. "Oh Millie, that would be wonderful, don't you agree?"

Mildred nodded. "Yes, I think it would be marvelous, if we can get some rest before hand."

Abigail tapped her fingertips together. "Yea! Millie, let's go back to our cabin and take a nap. Ferdinand, we can meet you about six here in the dining hall. Would that be okay?"

"That will be most wonderful."

He walked them to their door, bowed and said, "I look forward to our next meeting. Rest well, charming ladies."

Chapter 7

A Short Nap

Yawns and groans greeted the sound of their alarm clock.

"Abby, call Ferdinand and tell him we've changed our minds."

"Don't be silly dear, it'll just take a few minutes for us to get fully awake."

Mildred rubbed her eyes and moaned. "What was I thinking when I agreed to this?"

"Well, Millie, I think, you were thinking, 'Wouldn't it be wonderful to have an evening of dancing?' Besides, I don't know how to call him." She chuckled and added, "Millie, how would you feel about us taking a shower and then going to the hair salon? We could get our hair styled, as well as taking our makeup to let them do a makeover for us. And I think we should splurge on a new dinner outfit for this evening. What we have would do, of course, but this is our first time to take a cruise, let's get all-dolled-up for a change. What do you say?"

"I think that's a grand idea, Abby."

Abigail reached for the phone and punched in the numbers from the menu beside the bed. "Yes, this is Abigail Fine. I would like to make appointments for myself and my sister for hair and makeup sessions. Yes, we can be there in an hour. Thank you so much!" She replaced the receiver and smiled at her sister. "Who showers first?"

Mildred threw back the cover, sat up and kicked her legs off the bed. "Me! I'll only be a moment."

Reclining again, Abigail folded her hands behind her head and hummed, while swaying her shoulders into her pillow.

The water turned off and a shout from the bathroom came. "Abby, what do you think we should wear to the salon?"

"Something nice I suppose, but casual. We'll be stopping by the clothing shop on our way back, so we don't want to be too dowdy."

With a towel wrapped around her, Mildred cracked the bathroom door, steam rolled into the sleeping area. She looked at Abigail, still in bed. "Let's get a move on, Sleeping Beauty. We don't want to be late this evening."

Abigail slid from the covers and her feet hit the floor. "You're right. We want to have plenty of time for dancing." She hummed as she passed her sister.

"What's that you're humming?'

"I think it's 'Red Sails in the Sunset.'iii Very appropriate, don't you agree?"

The salon sparkled with glass and mirrors all around. Two lovely girls escorted them past the white basins, since their hair was still wet from their showers and seated them in adjacent chairs.

"Hi, I'm Shell." A beautiful girl with long blonde hair, stood behind Mildred.

A girl with shoulder-length dark, brown hair stood behind Abigail. "And I'm Becca, Ms. Fine."

Combing Mildred's hair back away from her face with her fingers, Shell asked, "What type of styles are you looking for this afternoon?"

Mildred began describing her usual style, but Abigail interrupted. "No Millie, let's be more adventurous than that. She stared into the mirror at her stylist's reflection. "What would you like to see done to me? We'll place ourselves in your hands."

The girl smiled back at the mirror. "Hmmm, okay, let's try this."

Mildred's stylist looked into the glass as well. "And you, ma'am, will you place yourself in my hands?"

"Indeed, I shall. Let's see what you can make of this old mug," and she laughed.

The stylists turned both chairs away from the mirrors, with their backs to each other.

An hour later, their hair had been styled and makeup applied. Neither lady had seen herself or her sister. When the final stroke of mascara was applied, the stylists looked at each other, nodded and turned the chairs so Mildred and Abigail could see each other.

Mildred saw Abigail first and gasped. "Abby!"

With eyes clinched tight, she said, "Oh dear, is it that bad?" Then she opened her eyes to see her sister. "Oh, Millie!"

The chairs then spun toward the mirrors.

Their mouths were already open, otherwise their jaws would have dropped.

Abigail eyed her reflection. "Oh, my goodness! Is that me?" Her focus shifted to the adjoining station. "Millie, you're gorgeous! It's like looking at you before your wedding, nearly fifty years ago."

Mildred shifted her glance to her sister's mirror. "And you look like a movie star, Abby! What miracles have these girls worked here today?"

They each raised their eyes to the reflection of the stylist standing behind them.

Becca chuckled and said, "Ladies, if you would force your chins up off of your chests, you would be even more stunning," and she smiled.

Mildred stared at her own reflection again. Her silver, curly hair cascaded in loops in the back, from the crown of her head, down to her collar. The top and sides flowed smooth and soft, at an angle toward the front and sides of her face. Soft wispy bangs touched her eyebrows. Subtle makeup brightened her face, with flattering colors that highlighted her eyes and her lips. "I can't believe this is me! What did you do with the old lady who sat down in your chair?"

Shell laughed. "To start with, I never saw an old lady, I saw a beautiful woman who no longer thought of herself as beautiful. I merely carved away the unbelief."

Mildred laughed. "Well dearie, I think you're a miracle worker." She turned her gaze to Abigail's mirror. "What do you think of yourself, sis?"

Abigail's short, perky hair framed her face with a pixie-like effect. It was still gray, but shone under the salon lights like spun silver, coming to a point on each cheek, near the bottom of her ears. Her eyes gleamed with contrasting eyeshadow and navy-blue mascara. The effect was dramatic, but still not overwhelming. "Millie, I can't believe the way either of us look. I don't think this is a beauty salon, I think it's a time machine."

Both stylists laughed from behind them.

Shell patted Mildred on the shoulder. "You ladies

take a moment. We'll be right back."

Still staring in unbelief at their reflections, Abigail finally spoke. "Millie, we need to go straight to the shipboard shop and find something dazzling to wear. We'll strike Ferdinand speechless."

"I like that, speechless would definitely be different." Millie tossed her head back and laughed. "If that old booger is up to no-good, let's make it as difficult for him as we can." She pulled the Velcro loose at the back of her cape and stood.

The two young women returned.

Shell said, "Ladies, we were about to place your charges on your room bill, but were told it would be taken care of," she squinted and craned her head forward, "by a Mr. Cranky Pants."

Mildred howled with laugher. "That old blighter really gets around. I'm beginning to like him more and more. What do you think, Abby?"

"I think he's going to add it to our house repair bill."

Mildred laughed. "Oh, don't be silly. Let's go find some exquisite clothes for tonight.

Abby's stylist, piped in. "We have also been given

strict instructions to accompany you and be sure you are immaculately attired."

Abigail wrinkled her nose. "Who gave you instructions?"

"I'm afraid that I'm not at liberty to say, ma'am, but again, place yourselves in our hands." She nodded to the other stylist. "Isn't that right, Shell?"

Mildred looked at Abigail then back to the girls. "Lead on!"

At the dress shop, chrome fixtures with soft lights illuminated the area. Rack upon rack of gorgeous clothing jiggled slightly as the ship steamed its way toward the Caribbean. Velvety, white cushioned ottomans offered a place to rest for any weary shoppers or admirers. A triple-paned mirror graced the corner of the room and reflected light all around.

Abigail spun before her full reflection. "I can't believe this. Who knew that I would look good in a midnight blue chiffon pantsuit with butterfly sleeves. Millie," she giggled, "you should have the butterfly sleeves."

At that moment, Mildred stepped from the dressing room and there was almost total silence in the shop, only the hum of the ship's engine could be heard. She proceeded toward the mirror and her mouth dropped open again. "Abby, these girls have worked another miracle." Trim black satin pants, topped with a tush-length clingy, red knit blouse caressed her body, as if it had been tailored for her. "I haven't worn anything clingy in decades." She turned to view her backside.

Abigail's mouth dropped open too. "Millie, where's your tummy pouch?"

She laughed. "These girls gave me this soft, rubber tube with leg holes to squeeze into and look, I'm flat as a pancake."

"Is it uncomfortable, dear?"

"No actually, once I wiggled into it, it felt very light and supportive. I feel wonderful." She turned to her sister. "What do you say we go give old Ferdinand a night of dancing he'll never forget?"

They entered the dining hall and heads turned from every direction. A familiar, friendly voice greeted them from behind. "Ladies," they turned to see Captain Williams, "may I take the liberty of saying that you look stunning."

Mildred laughed. "Yes, feel free, Captain Baby."

"Then I'm pleased to say that you are both—stunning. May I have a Captain's picture taken with you?" He motioned for a photographer to join them. "This will be one for my Hall of Fame." He stood between them and smiled.

The camera flashed.

Abigail laughed. "I see stars."

The Captain leaned in and whispered between them. "So, do I, now go sparkle on all the other passengers."

Abigail giggled. "Oh, Jeremiah, you're so sweet."

The ladies headed to the buffet line.

All of a sudden, Ferdinand was next to them. "Ladies, you look magnificent. I hope each of you plans to save a dance for me."

Mildred turned a most glamourous smile at him. "Oh, we plan to dance the night away, if you can keep up with us, Ferdinand."

His face went blank for a second, then he recovered

and nodded. "I will do my best, Ms. Butterfly."

All of the tables with a sea view were taken, but a suitable table overlooking the fantail became available. "Ladies, may I seat you?"

To Abigail's surprise, Ferdinand seated Mildred first, then scurried to her side of the table.

"Ms. Fine, may I say you look just that, fine, tonight?"

The gleam in her eyes disappeared. "Thank you, Ferdinand, but I can't hold a candle to my sister, as you can see. Isn't she gorgeous?"

"You both look splendid, madam."

In her usual direct manner, Mildred, dove in. "Let's eat, so I can start dancing. I want to work up a sweat before we stroll in the moonlight."

"Oh, Millie! You look so glamorous, don't spoil it by opening your mouth."

A huge belly laugh erupted from Mildred. "Very well, dear. I shall be the silent objet d'art."

Ferdinand's eyes flashed toward Mildred. "You, too, speak French, Ms. Butterfly?"

She cut her eyes toward him in an alluring manner. "Oui, as you said, it is the language of love."

Abigail plopped her elbow onto the table and leaned her cheek against her fist. "Isn't this a nice dinner?"

Mildred snickered. "Eat up, dearie," she winked, "so we can devour Ferdinand on the dance floor."

Only small talk transpired during dinner, but after the last morsel was finished, Ferdinand asked, "Shall we retire to the Main Rotunda for dancing, ladies?" He stepped around the table to assist Mildred with her chair, then returned to Abigail's side, but she had already scrapped her chair back. He offered her his elbow, she accepted, but with a straight face. He advanced toward Mildred, who turned away to walk in front of them.

The rotunda in the daytime was bright, airy and sparkling clean, with a large open area at the foot of the stairs, but for the dance, the top of the handrail of the semi-circular staircase had been laced with white roses and greenery. Each of the twenty-five marble stairs had a string of lights tucked into the crease between the tread and riser, they provided some light to walk-by, but also offered an illusion of descending from the clouds.

As they stepped onto the floor, a moving-portrait unfolded before them, lovely couples in beautiful attire, spun and swayed to romantic music across the expanse of the space.

Abigail walked to the outer rim of the room and chose a seat.

Mildred asked, "Would you hold my purse dear?" And tossed it on the seat next to her sister. She stepped forward and offered her hand to Ferdinand. "Shall we."

He bowed slightly, took her fingertips in his hand and led her to the edge of the dancing mass of people.

She started with a flourish of her hand and curtsied.

He smiled and placed one hand at her waist, lifting her other hand high and began to back her into the crowd in a waltz.

Before long, couple after couple gave way to their spectacular display of grace and poise.

"Ms. Butterfly, you did not tell me that you had been a professional dancer."

"Don't be silly, Ferdinand. I merely waltzed at parties with my husband, Maxwell. He was a large man, but surprisingly agile when it came to dancing. It was our favorite pastime."

The song ended and couples began to applaud.

Mildred realized they were in the center of the room. Her face flashed hot. "You need to go dance with Abigail now. I'll rest for a moment."

Ferdinand escorted her to the ring of seats surrounding the edge of the rotunda and offered his hand to Abigail.

She looked up, but her face reflected no joy. "Are you sure you wouldn't like to dance again with Millie?"

Mildred turned with delighted zeal, picked up her purse and positioned herself next to her sister. "Go ahead, Abby, enjoy the evening."

Abigail placed her fingers on Ferdinand's open palm. "Very well."

Once the music started, her face lit-up with pleasure.

Mildred suddenly noticed Captain Williams working his way her direction.

"Ms. Butterfly, you astound me. Your grace is beyond description."

She snickered. "Thanks, Captain Baby," she patted

the chair next to her, "now take a seat."

As instructed, he politely seated himself. "I'm glad to see you're enjoying the evening, Ms. Butterfly."

"Thank you, Captain Baby," her face changed, her eyes were piercing, her jaw clenched, "but we need to talk."

His eyes reacted to the tone of her voice and his face turned her direction. "Talk about what, madam?"

She nodded toward the dance floor. "See that slippery eel, dancing with my sister?"

"Yes, I thought you were enjoying his company."

She wagged her head and frowned. "Not even an inkling."

"So, why do you … "

She interrupted his question. "That man is slimy. He's up to something, I'd wager my next meal on it and I'm determined to find out what it is and not allow him to hurt my sister. Abigail is a piece of work, but she's my sister and he'd better not mess with her if he knows what's good for him."

"Well, I see your dilemma, Ms. Butterfly."

She glanced at Jeremiah. "You can call me Millie,

Captain Baby," she smiled, "or call me Grumpy Britches." She turned her face toward the dance floor again. "That's what Abigail occasionally calls me and that's exactly the way," she pointed at Ferdinand, "that man makes me feel."

The Captain tipped his head back in delightful laughter. "I will settle for Millie, or I might be thrown overboard for rudeness. I can't imagine what people would think if I called you," he leaned toward her, "Grumpy Britches."

"Very well, but mark my words, Captain, that man is up to something."

He faced the dancers again. "How can I help?"

"If you would be so kind as to give me your cellphone number, so I can keep you apprised of any developments."

"My pleasure, Millie, may I see your phone."

She reached in her small clutch bag and pulled out a cellphone.

Jeremiah entered his number in her address book and also marked it I.C.E. "Don't hesitate to call on me at any time."

"Thank you, Jeremiah," she smiled at him. "I never had a son, but if I had, I would've loved for him to be just like you."

He smiled, stood and offered his hand. "May I have this dance?"

She returned his smile, stood and took his hand. After a whirl or two around the floor, she laughed. "You are the most charming man, Jeremiah, now go flatter some of the younger passengers."

He bowed. "Yes, ma'am, Millie." He smiled and tucked his hands behind him as he walked away.

Mildred watched as the crowd began to thin, then across the room she caught sight of Jeremiah speaking to a man in the shadows. Tall, lean and distinguished, he wore a white dinner jacket, not a uniform, but they appeared to be deep in conversation.

Abigail diverted her attention when she came floating up with her hands clasped under her chin. "Oh, Millie, I haven't had so much fun ... since ... since I don't know when. Let me sit down for a moment, Ferdinand and catch my breath."

"Very well, Ms. Fine." He turned to Mildred,

"Would Ms. Butterfly care for another turn?"

"No, I think I would like to take that stroll on the deck, when my sister has sufficiently recovered." She looked across the room again, but Jeremiah and the stranger had disappeared.

Abigail bolted from her chair. "I'm fine, Millie, let's go chase a little moonlight."

"Very well, dear. Ferdinand, would you lead the way?"

Chapter 8

The Stroll

Abigail walked alongside Ferdinand and hooked her hand around his elbow, his forearm instantly pulled into position to accommodate her. She tipped her head up to drink-in the light of the full moon. "This is the most magical time I've had since my honeymoon with Henry. That man delighted me so much, he was always full of fun and surprises. I've missed that more than I realized."

Ferdinand patted her hand. "You have been a blessed woman, Ms. Fine. One can tell just by meeting you that you have been well cared for and loved, you are so sweet and kind. It is my pleasure to provide an evening of entertainment for you," he looked behind them, "and for your sister, it's clear that she cares for you very much." He stopped and turned slightly, "Ms. Butterfly, would you like to take my other arm?"

"No, Ferdinand, dear. I'm perfectly content strolling behind the two of you."

He replied, "Is this something you and your husband enjoyed doing?"

She stopped and pushed her hands behind her back as she had seen the Captain do. "No, Ferdinand, we were pretty much home-bodies, except for waltzing at occasional affairs. I enjoyed his company, even when he said nothing. He made me feel accepted for who I was and loved beyond anything I could ever have imagined. He was an amazing man that most people overlooked, I suppose that's what made him such a good detective."

Even in the dim light, she could tell that his eyebrows jumped up. "A detective?"

She smiled. "Yes, my Maxwell and Abigail's husband, Henry owned a detective agency. They sometimes had horrible hours, but when they arrived home, we had their complete attention. Isn't that right, Abby?"

Glancing at Abigail, they both noticed the glistening of tears in her eyes. "Yes, Millie, that's so true, they were total opposites, yet so much alike. Henry was lean, athletic and handsome. He and Maxwell had been friends since childhood."

Mildred laughed. "You can go ahead and say it, Abby, Max was Henry's lumbering, over-weight best friend. In high school he was ridiculed because of his size and awkwardness, you can imagine the numerous butterfly jokes, considering him being such a big guy, but Henry leapt to his defense at every insult. The jocks used to refer to Max as Henry's DUFF, you know, designated ugly fat friend, but I think that's what made Maxwell so tender and gentle as an adult. He knew the hurt people could inflict on others and he hated it. It took him awhile to forgive his high school tormentors, but once he met the Lord, he broke free of the hurt of that abuse, he was the kindest, most compassionate, most understanding soul a person could ever want to meet and, in business, he refused to take any case involving a single one of his tormentors. He didn't want anyone to think it was revenge. He was my hero and the love of my life."

Abigail burst into tears. "Oh, Millie, I miss them both so much. They were such a good team, a true friendship, without an abundance of rules, they only wanted to love and be loved."

Mildred stepped to her side, opposite Ferdinand and wrapped her arm around her sister's shoulder. "Yes, dear, God truly blessed us with wonderful husbands."

They continued their walk, in silence, under the drenching rays of moonlight.

Chapter 9

Goodnight, Ladies

The stroll ended at the double doors of the passageway to their stateroom.

Abigail extended her hand. "Goodnight, Ferdinand. Thank you for the wonderful evening."

"It was indeed my pleasure, madam. You and your sister are enchanting dance partners. May I be so bold as to suggest an outing for tomorrow?"

She patted his hand. "Certainly, dear, what do you have in mind?"

"We will pull in to our first port tomorrow just after sunrise and I would like to make arrangements to show you the sights of that lovely city. May I hire a car and take you and your sister to some of my favorite places?"

She turned to her sister. "Millie, does that sound okay to you? I would like to go."

"Yes, that would be wonderful." Mildred smiled. "Having someone familiar with the city as a guide sounds delightful indeed."

"May I call for you at eight and we will have breakfast before we leave?"

Mildred sighed. "Can you come for us at nine o'clock, Ferdinand. It's late and we need to get our rest."

"Certainly, Ms. Butterfly. I will curb my enthusiasm, but until then, goodnight, dear ladies."

Mildred waved. "Goodnight, Mr. Modesto."

Abigail smiled. "Ta-ta! See you in the morning."

A few steps later, they reached their room, Mildred slid the key card over the sensor, turned the handle and the door swung inward. "Oh, Abby, I'm getting too old for this."

"Nonsense, dear. You were spectacular on the dance floor."

Mildred faced her and grinned. "We were both spectacular, dear. Ferdinand will drop into bed exhausted tonight." She laughed. "But I may need your help to wriggle out of this new undergarment."

Abigail smiled. "Let me take off my outfit and I'll be right with you." Abigail donned her night gown and swirled her shirt's butterfly sleeves as she waltzed her outfit to the closet. She crossed the floor again. "Tonight, was grand, simply grand." She stepped toward Mildred and reached for her sleeve, "Here let me help you."

Pulling the top over her head, Mildred tried not to muss-up her hair. "You know, Abby, you're right. It was grand and I felt like I did when Max was alive. I think we've both been depressed and this trip was a God-send."

"I think you're right, Millie, we've both been in a rut. I'm glad we're here, but I wish it hadn't taken a deluge in my kitchen to manage it."

Mildred sat on the edge of the bed and kicked-off her shoes, then stood and the satiny pants slipped off effortlessly. "Now, for this monstrosity around my middle." She began to roll it from under her breastbone, down over her ribs, to her hips and she suddenly shouted, "This thing zips-off like a banana peel! I'm amazed!"

Abigail added, "And it was so slimming, dear. You looked gorgeous tonight."

Mildred chuckled. "I did, didn't I? And you, Abby, so lovely. You turned heads all around the rotunda. I'm glad Mr. Greasy prodded us into high gear."

"Oh, Millie, don't call him that, so far he's been nothing but a gentleman."

"Okay, dearest, now let's wash off this lovely façade of makeup and get some sleep. It's two o'clock, when the alarm goes off at eight it's going to feel really early."

Chapter 10

The Beach

Her words were prophetic. When the alarm sounded, they both groaned.

"Oh, Abby, call Ferdinand and tell him we're going to sleep in."

Abigail pushed her feet off the bed. "Nonsense, now chop-chop and I've told you before, I don't know how to call him. I'll shower first. Will you pick out some casual clothing for us? And remember … "

The cover swung back. "Yeah, I know, not too matchy-matchy." So, this time she chose red capris for herself with a white, button-up, short-sleeved shirt. For Abigail she chose red capris and a white pull-over tank top.

Abigail entered the room wearing a robe. She looked at the clothes stretched out on the bed. "Honestly, Millie, you get more like mother every day."

As Mildred breezed past with her clothes in her hand, she said, "Thank you, dear, how sweet of you."

Forty-five minutes later, *tap, tap, tap.*

Abigail opened the door. "Good morning, Ferdinand."

"Good morning, Ms. Fine. I hope you and Ms. Butterfly slept well."

"We did indeed, but we are sorely in need of coffee."

Mildred emerged from the bathroom. Her hair was not quite as well coiffed as the night before. It stood slightly higher on the right side than on the left. "Good morning!" She reached for sunglasses and a large sunhat. "Shall we go and find that caffeine now?"

In the dining room, the crowd had thinned considerably. Ferdinand secured a table near the window, deposited cups of steaming coffee, then joined the ladies at the buffet. "The breakfast looks superb, wouldn't you agree?"

Abigail lifted a slice of meat from her plate. "This is the most, yummy bacon I've ever eaten."

The now familiar voice of Captain Williams approached from behind. "We have it specially sugar cured on a plantation near here. I would be glad to escort you for a tour."

Abigail turned. "Jeremiah, good morning. That sounds delightful, but we have plans with Ferdinand today. Have you two met?"

The Captain extended his hand. "No, I haven't had the pleasure."

Ferdinand reached for the outstretched hand and Abigail made the introduction. "Captain, this is Ferdinand Modesto. Ferdinand, this is our wonderful Captain, Jeremiah Williams."

Both men nodded and the handshake ended.

The Captain addressed Ferdinand. "Sir, you have the pleasure of escorting my two favorite passengers today." He looked to Mildred. "Ladies, I hope you have a wonderful day." He winked and turned to greet other passengers.

Mildred's face emitted her approval, followed by, "Now with pleasantries out of the way, shall we eat our breakfast?"

Ferdinand nodded. "Yes, we should. I would like to show you the beach this morning before the sun gets too hot for you fair ladies, then we can take a taxi to some nearby spots of interest."

Abigail agreed. "That's a good point. I don't want to burn on our first day ashore. We should also take bottles of water with us, we want to stay well hydrated."

After breakfast, they walked down the pier and stopped into a restaurant for a soft drink to take with them, they stepped out the back door onto the patio, but rather than being seated, it gave them access to the adjoining beach. "This is a little trick I've learned in my travels. A small drink to go and you can dispense with the taxi ride until you desire it."

Not yet ten o'clock, the sun already beat down blisteringly hot, so they strolled along under the edge of the palm trees and watched the waves.

Mildred reached in her big bag. "Abby, let me put

some sunscreen on you. Even with your hat on, your neck and arms are too exposed."

"Thank you, Millie. Now let me put some on you. And Ferdinand, do you need sunscreen?"

"Thank you, Ms. Fine. I will be ... "

Abigail laughed. "You'll be what? Fine?" She laughed again. "Will you please call me Abby?"

"Certainly, if you wish."

They continued their trek down the beach with Abigail holding Ferdinand's arm.

Mildred walked along beside her.

Abigail pushed her chin up to see out from under the wide brim of her hat. "Millie, what would you like for Ferdinand to call you?"

"Yes, please call me Princess Butterfly."

She swatted her sister's wrist. "Oh, Millie, behave."

They stopped and she turned toward Ferdinand. "I'm sorry, I think I'm a little sleep deprived this morning. Yes, please call me, Mildred. Only four people in the world have called me Millie; my late mother, my late husband, my sister and a new special friend."

He tipped his head. "Very well, Ms. Mildred. I

consider it an honor."

Scanning the sea, Abigail wiggled Ferdinand's arm. "Oh, look at the sailboat." She pointed, "I would love to go sailing."

"Then let's see if we can make that happen." Ferdinand led the way to a cabana. "Sir, can we book a tour on a sailboat this morning."

"Yes, there will be one leaving in five minutes. That will be forty dollars per person, please."

Ferdinand patted his pockets. "Ladies, I seem to have left my wallet in my cabin. I hate to disappoint you, but …"

Abigail reached for the small purse that hung across her body. "Nonsense, I'll be glad to pay for this. We will have a splendid time."

Mildred frowned, but held her tongue.

When Ferdinand glanced her way, she managed a smile.

They boarded the sailboat just before it pushed away from the small inland dock. They found deck chairs near the rail. A cool breeze from the sea wrestled the blazing sun.

Mildred fanned herself with the brochure they each received. "My, but it's hot."

Abigail tried to position the brim of her hat to its greatest effect. "All the other seats are taken, perhaps we should apply more sunscreen."

Mildred put down her make-shift fan. "Excellent idea, here let me help you."

After layers of lotion, Ferdinand offered to spread his jacket behind them as some relief.

Abigail tucked under the shade of his garment. "Thank you, dear, I must apologize, it seems this was not the best idea after all."

Mildred frowned. "Maybe when we head back to shore, the sail will offer some protection."

And so, it did.

***

Following the two-hour tour, Ferdinand suggested, "I'm sure you will both agree that our visit to the city should wait for tomorrow, is that okay with my lovely companions? It is already very hot, too hot I think for such gentle creatures to continue a tour," and he smiled.

Abigail took his arm and patted it. "That will be fine. We should return to the ship now for lunch and perhaps a nap, I'm exhausted."

He peered over at her and Mildred. "Would either of you be opposed to my making a reservation for dinner this evening for the three of us at a very nice restaurant? They have the most amazing lobster dishes on the island."

Abigail pulled her hand from his elbow and clamped them together lacing her fingers. "Millie, that sounds wonderful, don't you agree?"

She paused for a moment, as though cogs turned in her brain, but then she smiled. "Yes, dear, but we both need some rest first. We should return to the ship now, eat a light lunch, then retire for two or three-hours' rest."

Ferdinand smiled and nodded. "Splendid!"

When they arrived at the dining hall, several people were leaving just as they entered.

Abigail smiled at Ferdinand. "Will you get our drinks? I'll find a table and make a plate for myself and one for you."

"Certainly, Abby, that will be my pleasure."

It took several minutes longer than they imagined before he arrived with the drinks.

Abigail smiled. "We were worried about you. What took so long?"

He distributed the drinks around the table. "I took a moment to make dinner reservations for tonight and I hope both of you will join me for a moonlight stroll on the beach afterwards."

Abigail stared into Ferdinand's eyes. "We would love too, isn't that right, Millie?"

Without looking, she assumed Mildred's eyes bore down on her neck, but rather than a stern rebuke, she heard, "Yes, that would be very nice. Thank you, Ferdinand, we would love to join you."

Abigail swished her head toward Mildred and glared at her sister, but added, "Yes, that will be wonderful."

The light lunch was quickly consumed.

Ferdinand stood. "May I escort you back to your room?"

Mildred cast the most pleasant smile his direction.

"That is so thoughtful of you, Ferdinand, but I think we'll take a short walk around the fantail first, you know to settle our meal, then we'll rest before we dress for dinner. Will you call for us at our room again this evening?"

"Certainly, madam, shall we say six o'clock? That will give us time to depart the ship and make our way to the restaurant in time for our reservation."

Mildred smiled. "Wonderful, we'll see you at six."

Ferdinand stood and tipped his head. "I look forward to the pleasure."

As he repaired from the table, Abigail leaned across on her elbows. "What are you up to, Millie?"

She grinned at her perplexed sister. "Nothing, dear, I merely see the fun of having an escort and a chaperone to go ashore with us."

"I don't believe you, Millie," she smiled, "but I do agree that it'll be nice to have a gentleman with us this evening. Now let's take a walk around. We need to see more of the boat than the dining room and our cabin."

They left through the rear door and bumped straight into Captain Williams. "Hello, ladies, how is your trip so far?"

Abigail launched in. "You have the most scrumptious food and our stateroom is lovely. We were about to walk around and tour the back part of the ship."

"It would be my pleasure to accompany you on your ramblings and I wondered, if you don't have any plans this evening, would you like to dine with me at the Captain's Table?"

Mildred grinned. "We had planned to roam about on our own, Captain Baby, and as for the dinner invitation, that would have been a pleasure, but we have just accepted an offer to dine ashore with Ferdinand. Maybe tomorrow night or the next, if that's convenient for you."

"Certainly, ladies. I'm glad you are making friends and enjoying yourselves." He winked but only Mildred saw it. "I will leave you to your rambling, but if you ever need anything, please don't hesitate to ask." He removed his hat, tucked it under his arm, smiled and entered the dining room.

Abigail smiled after him. "What a gracious man! If I were twenty years younger."

"Oh, Abby, for Pete's Sake! Come on, let's get back to our room."

"But Millie, I thought we were going to explore the ship."

"We'll have time for that later, right now we need to pray and we need to make a plan."

Chapter 11

Planning

Back in their room, Abigail sat down on the bed. "What do you mean, we need to make a plan?"

"Abby, I don't intend to let that guy get away with whatever he has up his sleeve."

"Oh, surely by now you can see that he doesn't have anything up his sleeve, Millie."

"Honestly, Abby, you are so gullible. Didn't you see how he conveniently," she crooked two fingers of each hand to make air-quotation marks, "he forgot his wallet?"

Abigail lifted her shoulders and her palms turned up. "That can happen to anyone."

"Well, we're going to put it to the test."

"How?"

"This evening when he picks us up for dinner, Abby, I want you to leave your purse here, but ask Mr. Greasy to put your credit card in his pocket in case of an emergency."

"Oh, Millie, you're outrageous. What will that accomplish?"

"I have my suspicions about this guy. Tonight, he'll either prove me right or prove me wrong, in the meantime, this should make you happy."

"What's that?"

"Let's see if we can get appointments to get our hair styled again and buy some superb dresses for this evening."

Abigail dove across the bed for the phone and tapped in the extension numbers. "Yes, this is Abigail Fine, can my sister and I get appointments again for this afternoon with the same stylists we had yesterday, Shell and Becca? — Wonderful! — Yes, four o'clock will be perfect."

Mildred smiled. "Now, Abby, we need to get a couple of hours of rest."

Abigail sat up on the bed. "I'm too excited to sleep."

Mildred stretched out. "Well, keep it down so I can." She pulled the bedspread over her and her eyes clamped shut immediately. She knew Abigail would drift off eventually.

Three o'clock, the alarm sounded.

Mildred fumed and flopped her arms out on top of the duvet. "Oh, heavens, when am I going to stop having these brilliant ideas? Why can't we just rest on this cruise?"

Abigail flung the covers back. "Oh pish-posh, I'll shower first. And you can …"

"I know, pick out some outfits. What about what we wore to the beach this morning, since we're going to buy new dresses anyway?"

"Okay, that will do."

Abigail finished showering and dressed while Mildred showered. When Mildred had finished in the bathroom, Abigail said, "Millie, I'm going to pack just the makeup they used on us yesterday. No need to take the whole kit'n kaboodle. I'm glad the girls had our casual clothes and cosmetics brought to the room. In fact, everything is still in the little bag they provided."

"That's fine with me. I've finished my shower. Would you hand me my clothes? I'll get dressed and we'll have just enough time to get to the salon for our appointment."

Chapter 12

The Hair Salon

"Hello, ladies, it's nice to see you again. We've heard reports that you danced the night away into the wee hours of the morning."

Mildred laughed. "Who told you that?"

"Aww, madam, we have our sources." Shell chuckled. "What are your plans for this evening? Shall we do the same as yesterday? Or a little more dramatic for this evening?"

Mildred glanced at her sister's image. "I think the same as yesterday will suit me just fine. What about you, Abby?"

Her sister giggled. "We're going to the Savoy for dinner tonight, girls." She put her finger to her chin.

"Hmmm, how dramatic are we talking?"

Both stylists laughed and Becca said, "You trusted us yesterday, why don't you do it again?"

Abigail nodded. "Go for it!" and she pointed to Millie, "and dramatic her up too."

Mildred frowned. "Abigail! Really!"

Only an hour later and the chairs were spun toward the mirrors.

Abigail leaned toward her reflection. "Who is that?"

Mildred pitched forward too. "Forget her, who is this over here?"

They looked at each other's reflection, then at their stylists.

Mildred asked, "Girls, are you sure about this?"

Shell bent close to her ear. "Indeed, we are. With the right dress and shoes, you two will be dynamite! Now off we go to the dress shop."

Minutes later Abigail stood before the mirror, dressed in a fitted, floor length, sky blue, sequined dress with a short bolero jacket. Her hair was pulled behind one ear and dramatically pointed on the other cheek. Her eyes shimmered with midnight blue eyeshadow and mascara. "I can't believe it. I can't even decide if I like it, it's so different."

Mildred's voice behind her caused her to stop. "You're a vision, Abigail, if Henry could see you now."

"Oh, Millie, don't make me cry."

One of the girls handed her a tissue. "Blot, don't wipe."

"And you! Look at you! Millie, come stand here." She stepped away from the mirror to make room.

Mildred stepped in. "I'm flabbergasted. Are you sure this looks okay?"

Her stylist stepped up behind her. "No, ma'am, it doesn't look okay, it looks spectacular."

Her hair was blown out fluffy, with some waves all the way around and swept behind her ear on the side with the part, only a few wispy pieces covered that ear. Little flippy, wings of hair broke the smoothness here and there, but in just the right places. Her eyeshadow was a deep burgundy, to match the sequined gown she wore. The sweetheart neckline gave her a delicate, feminine appearance.

"Millie, you look like a queen."

"Oh, Abby, don't be silly."

"I'm not, dear, I promise."

Becca said, "Ladies, we will return your other clothes to your room. Now you need to go meet your king."

For the first time, Mildred frowned. "King, huh. He's more like a frog wanting to be kissed. And he's picking us up at our stateroom, so we can handle our duds this time. Thanks, sweeties."

The girls laughed. "Then go make him jealous."

Chapter 13

Back at the Room

"Abby, do you have your bright gold Visa card?"

"Yes, but I still don't understand why I'm leaving my purse here. What if I need a comb or lipstick?"

"I have a comb and I'll put your lipstick in my purse."

"Then why don't you carry the credit card."

"Oh Abigail!"

Tap, tap, tap.

She whispered, "Just do what I tell you, now answer the door."

A smile swept across Abigail's face as the door swung inward. "Ferdinand."

His mouth dropped open and he was speechless.

She grinned at him. "Well, dear, are you ready to go ashore?"

"Ms. Abby, you're lovely." He looked behind her. "And Ms. Mildred, you are a vision."

Mildred walked forward and batted her eyes. "Thank you, Ferdinand, shall we go?"

"Oh, and Abby doesn't want to carry a purse tonight, so …"

Abigail lifted her Visa card and asked, "Would you mind carrying my credit card, just in case of emergencies, you understand."

He slid it in behind his handkerchief, "I will guard it with my life," and patted his pocket.

Mildred laughed. "No need to go that far, dear."

He opened the door and they strolled down the corridor. Reaching the exit adjacent to the gangway, Ferdinand pushed it open to find Captain Williams standing near the stairs.

"Ms. Fine, Ms. Butterfly and Mr. Modesto, I see you are off for an unforgettable evening and may I compliment you on your appearances. I've not seen more beautiful women in my life," he leaned forward and whispered, "but don't tell my wife I said that," his smile charmed them to the core.

Mildred lifted her hand so he could assist her onto the stairs. "Yes, Captain Williams, this night holds much promise. Please, leave a light on for us, but don't wait up," she grinned.

He tossed his head back and laughed. "You ladies are a delight."

They walked down the stairs to the pier, there a car waited. Ferdinand opened the rear door. Abigail entered first and slid to the middle. Mildred sat down and swiveled her knees in behind the driver.

Ferdinand closed her door, then rushed to the other side and climbed in. "To the Savoy, driver."

A short drive landed them in front of a large restaurant with twinkling lights around the sign. The driver stayed behind the wheel and Ferdinand got out and stretched his hand toward Abigail. "Ms. Abby." When she stood, he rushed to the other side, opened the door and offered his hand. "Ms. Mildred."

The driver turned for his payment.

Ferdinand asked, "Ladies, do either of you have a twenty? I don't have anything smaller than a hundred-dollar bill."

Mildred reached in her purse and pulled out a twenty.

"Thank you, Ms. Mildred. I will repay you."

He ushered her around toward her sister and stepped between them, lifting his elbows on each side.

At the entrance, a doorman opened the door.

Ferdinand pulled his elbow from Abigail's hand and gestured for her to go ahead, then he did the same for Mildred.

The maître d' met them inside. "Good evening, do you have a reservation?"

His smooth male voice answered. "Yes, Modesto, for three."

The restaurant glittered with marble floors and twinkling lights with crystal stars decorated the ceiling. Potted plants separated the spaces and each table was lit by a single, Moravian Star hung directly overhead.

The man consulted his list. "Very good, sir, our finest table, this way please."

As they passed-by occupied tables, iridescent

champagne-colored tablecloths shimmered in the candlelight from the centerpieces. Through the tall windows, flames of torches on the beach danced in the wind.

The maître d' pulled a chair out for Mildred and Ferdinand did the same for Abigail. "Please, enjoy your evening."

Abigail glanced around. "Oh, Ferdinand, this is so elegant."

"Nothing but the best for you, charming ladies."

The waiter approached. "The wine list, sir."

Mildred waved him off. "No, thank you."

"As you wish madam," he turned abruptly.

Ferdinand asked, "You do not wish wine with dinner?"

In her direct manner, Mildred answered, "No, I can't stand the stuff and it gives Abigail hives."

"Oh, I'm sorry to hear that, but of course I shall not have any either."

He snapped his fingers. "Waiter, menu please." It was presented, wine glasses removed and water glasses filled.

"Ladies, this restaurant is renowned for its lobster dishes. I have tried several if you would like any recommendations."

Mildred stared at the list. "I think I see exactly what I want already. What about you, Abby?"

"Oh, I'm not sure, what would you recommend, Ferdinand? I don't want to have to wrestle with a lobster shell in this dress."

He glanced over the top of his page. "Lobster Newberg is a particular favorite of mine."

"Hmmm, that sounds yummy."

Again, the fingers snapped. "Garcon, we are ready to order. Ms. Mildred, what would you like?"

"I'll have the lobster salad, with a cup of lobster bisque and do you have sweet tea?"

"Yes, madam." The waiter looked up, "and for the other lady?"

"She and I will both have the Lobster Newberg, with some of your fresh baked bread and sweet tea."

"Yes, sir, right away."

Ferdinand leaned on one elbow. "It will take a few minutes, as the items are prepared especially for each customer."

Abigail was swaying to the music. "It's too bad we can't dance here, the music is lovely."

Ferdinand's lips pulled a little to one side. "Who says we cannot dance?"

"But no one else is dancing."

He pushed his chair back and reached for her hand.

"I can't, Ferdinand."

He leaned forward. "Maybe if we dance, others will catch the passion."

She shook her head. "No, not here."

"Very well," he took his seat again.

Mildred leaned her wrists onto the table. "Tell us again, what line of work you are in Ferdinand, I believe you said acquisitions."

"Yes, it is very boring to most people, but I love the travel."

"What do you acquire exactly?"

"Well, madam, it depends on what is wanted at the time."

"Who are your clients?"

"Different individuals, at different times."

"What's the most unusual thing you have acquired?"

The waiter served three glasses of sweet tea, then stepped away.

"Hmmm, that would probably be very boring for you madam." Ferdinand looked away and motioned for the musician to come to the table. "For you, ladies."

A handsome young man with a guitar came directly to the table. He stood next to Mildred, the music was so loud, it was impossible to talk, but with eyes closed, Abigail swayed to the rhythmic strumming.

The waiter arrived with a tray, forcing the musician to step away. "The lobster salad and bisque, for madam and two servings of Lobster Newberg with a basket of warm bread. Will there be anything else?" He scanned their faces.

Ferdinand nodded. "We will call you if we need anything."

Mildred startled Ferdinand when she asked, "Would you bless the food?"

He stammered, "Perhaps you would prefer to, Ms. Mildred."

She began to pray. "Father, thank you for this

wonderful food and direct our paths this evening. In Jesus' name. Amen."

Abigail leaned in to smell her food. "Thank you, Millie, and this smells scrumptious."

He motioned toward the bread basket. "May I break some bread for you ladies?"

Abigail grinned and placed her hands in her lap. "Yes, please."

Ferdinand took the napkin and the bread from the basket and broke off a portion, being careful not to touch it with his bare hands. He held the napkin toward Abigail who reached up and took a piece, then he broke another piece and turned the loaf to Mildred.

She took a piece and smiled. "Thank you, Ferdinand."

Abigail smelled the crusty bread. "Hmmm, this is fresh from the oven." She placed it on the rim of her bowl, took her spoon and scooped away from herself. A large piece of lobster claw rested in the spoon. "Here we go." She placed the bite into her mouth, chewed and sighed. "Oh, my goodness this is good."

"I'm delighted you like it." Ferdinand took a big

scoop. "Yes, just as I remembered, delicious. Ms. Mildred, how is your meal?"

"I can't decide which word to use. Scrumptious? Delicious? Or delightful?"

He smiled. "Maybe all three would work well."

"Yes, I believe you're right," she smiled.

"And Ms. Abby, if you take your piece of bread to assist getting the food into the spoon," he demonstrated, "it absorbs some of the sauce. All one can do at that point is to eat it," he grinned.

She swiped a piece of bread into the bowl, pushing morsels and sauce onto her spoon, then raised it to her mouth, chewed and swallowed. Following that she ate the soaked bread. "Hmmm, yes, I see what you mean. This is amazing."

Ferdinand gestured and the musician returned to the table, so not much conversation took place, but the food was elegantly devoured, down to and including the last crust of bread.

Mildred sat straight in her chair and dabbed the corners of her mouth with her napkin. "That was one of the most delicious meal I've ever eaten. The lobster pieces were sweet and juicy, the salad dressing was light and fresh, very flavorful, but not overwhelming."

"I am so glad, madam."

Mildred pushed back her chair. "Perhaps Abby and I should visit the Ladies' Room before we set out to stroll on the beach." She nodded at her sister. "Come along, Abby, dear."

Ferdinand stood.

The ladies rose and headed toward the facilities, but before they reached them, Mildred yanked Abigail behind a large potted plant and scrunched down.

She whispered, "What are we doing, Millie?"

"Watch and learn."

They saw Ferdinand snap his fingers. The waiter brought the bill to the table on a small silver tray. Ferdinand reached into his breast pocket and pulled out a shiny, gold card.

Abigail shot up straight. "That's *my* Visa card!"

"Shhh, yes, I'm afraid it is, dear, now scrunch back down, so he won't see you."

She did, as instructed and whispered, "What are we going to do, Millie?"

"Nothing yet, but we are going to teach that gigolo a lesson. Now let's go back to the table and tell him that you are becoming itchy, that perhaps there was some wine in the Lobster Newberg sauce and we need to return to the ship, but first we'll stay here until he signs the bill."

As soon as the waiter took the signed bill, Ferdinand popped the gold card back into his breast pocket.

Mildred straightened and beckoned for Abby to follow, they stepped from behind the potted plant and casually made their way to the table.

Abigail rubbed her arms. "Ferdinand, I'm starting to itch. I'm afraid I'm having a reaction to the lobster sauce, maybe it contained wine."

He stood. "Do we need to take you to the hospital?"

"No, it's not that severe, but I need to return to the ship and take some medication."

He stood with wide eyes. "Certainly, dear lady."

He escorted them to the front door and asked the doorman to call for a cab.

A sharp whistle, produced a taxi at the curb immediately and they made the short trip back to the ship.

The driver opened the rear door for Mildred and Abigail, who stepped out and immediately headed up the stairs. He then turned to Ferdinand for payment.

Mildred yelled back over her shoulder. "We'll see you tomorrow, Ferdinand. I'm going to get Abby to the room."

They walked up the stairs, where Jeremiah was waiting. "Is everything alright, ladies?"

They peered over the rail to see Ferdinand pull the card from his breast pocket again, but the driver waved it off. They weren't sure what all was said, but Ferdinand removed his watch from his wrist. The driver flapped his arms, but took it.

Millie pointed over the rail. "Captain Baby, we're going to teach that man a lesson," then they scurried away toward their stateroom, before Ferdinand topped the stairs.

Chapter 14

The Lesson Begins

In their suite, Abigail frantically asked, "Millie, what am I going to do about my credit card? What if he tries to use it again?"

"You can call the company right now, they have a twenty-four-hour, toll-free line and you can ask them to accept the charge to the Savoy," her eyes met her sister's, "we don't want the restaurant to be cheated because of that man, then ask them to place a freeze on the account and not allow any charges after that until we call them again."

"I'm glad you're so level-headed, Millie. You saw straight through Mr. Greasy-slicky-slimy-oily-Modesto. What would I do without you?"

"Hey, I may give you a hard time, but nobody else is allowed to," she smiled at her sister.

Abigail picked up her cell phone and found the number for the Visa company. "I'm glad Simone took care of getting me that International plan." She placed the call and explained the situation exactly as Mildred had told her.

After she hung up, Mildred gave her a hug. "Don't worry now, Abby, we'll get the card back tomorrow and if we don't, he can't use it anyway. Let's get out of these beautiful dresses and wash away the night's drama," she smiled, "starting with our makeup, then we'll get a good night's sleep."

Chapter 15

At Breakfast

The next morning, they entered the dining room around eight-thirty, Mildred spotted the Captain and waved for him to come to their table.

"Good morning, ladies. I hope you slept well."

Smiling, Mildred patted the table. "We did, Captain Baby, thank you, but do you have time to join us, we have a tale to tell?"

He pulled out a chair and sat. "I knew something was up last night, but I figured you'd share when you were ready."

Abigail started. "I should've listened to my sister, believe me, I've learned my lesson. Millie was right all along about Mr. Modesto."

The Captain leaned in. "How do you mean?"

"Millie summed him up in two seconds and she was right. He's a greasy, oily, slimy …"

Mildred interrupted. "Yes dear, Jeremiah gets the picture."

Abigail balled up her fists on the table in front of her and leaned toward the Captain. "He's a gigolo! Our dinner bill last night with the tip was probably over two hundred dollars and that worm put it on my credit card when he thought we weren't looking."

Jeremiah's forehead wrinkled. "How did he get your credit card?"

Abigail smiled at her sister. "Oh, that was part of Millie's plan. I told him I didn't want to carry a purse and asked him to put my card in his pocket, in case of an emergency."

The Captain's voice softened. "Do you think that was wise? What if he uses it again?"

Abigail faced him. "Oh, Millie's brilliant. She had me call and tell the credit card company to place a hold on the card, but after the restaurant bill appeared, of course." Her forehead wrinkled. "We didn't want them to get caught up in part of our *sting.*"

He laughed. "You two magnificent ladies are a class act." He leaned in again and grinned. "I hope this isn't insulting, because I mean it in the kindest way imaginable, you remind me of my mother," and he winked at Mildred.

Her eyebrows rose and she leaned back. "That is the kindest thing you could ever had said, Jeremiah."

"Now girls, what's your next move?"

Mildred leaned her elbows on the table and grinned. "I thought we might want to go on a shopping trip."

Jeremiah leaned back and laughed. "Remind me to never rub you two the wrong way. Just keep me apprised of your doings and please be careful."

Mildred leaned to the center of the table and whispered, "Captain Baby, do you have a gun?"

His eyes flew open and his mouth dropped.

She continued, "Because if you do, keep it away from me or I'll shoot that gigolo in the rump!"

Jeremiah straightened his back and burst out laughing. "Oh, my gracious! You are delightful!" He pushed his chair back, stood, but leaned down and placed his hands on the table. "Girls, I mean it, be careful and keep me informed of your every move."

Mildred stood. "I think I feel a shopping trip coming on, Captain Baby." She smiled and said, "and then a lazy day of sunning at a bar on the beach."

Jeremiah laughed again. "Oh, my, do I need to plan to send a shuttle to pick you up?"

A wide grin filled her cheeks. "No dear, we don't drink."

Chapter 16

A Note

When they arrived back at their room, a sticky note clung to the door.

Mildred pulled the note free. "Mr. Greasy stopped by to see how you were doing, Abby. When we weren't here, he went to the infirmary to see if you were there, then came back here to leave us a note."

"That was nice of him." She balled up her fists and shook her head. "Oh, what am I saying? He's not nice."

"Right dear, he just doesn't want to lose a couple of big fish, so he was checking on you. The note asks us to call him and here's his number." She turned the paper to face her sister. "Would you like to phone him, or shall I?"

"You call him, Millie. You're so clever."

"First, we need to pray." They went in, sat on the foot of the bed and clasped hands. "Father it's no surprise to you that we are here and that we have run afoul of Mr. Greasy, now we need your guidance. What would you have us do, Father? In Jesus' name. Amen."

Mildred opened her eyes and chuckled. "Yes, I know exactly what to say." She picked up the cabin phone and dialed. "Hello, Ferdinand, dear. — Yes, we found your note. Abigail slept soundly, once the itch subsided. — No, dear, other than that, we had a wonderful time last night. We went for a light breakfast and just returned to find your note and we're feeling grand. In fact, I have an idea. I feel a shopping trip coming on. Yesterday, before our wonderful sailboat excursion, I saw a shop called the Beach Comber. It had these wonderful swimsuits in the window. I haven't even owned a bathing suit in years, but I would like to buy one and then go to the beach. What do you say? — That's wonderful, oh and Ferdinand, neither of us are taking our purses," she winked at Abigail, "so bring lots of small bills," she paused, "and a few large ones too. — Yes, call for us now if you like. I want to get in plenty of beach time in before lunch."

Only moments later, *tap, tap, tap.*

Wearing no makeup and with hair dried into natural curls, Mildred opened the door. "Good morning, Ferdinand." She turned toward the bathroom. "Abby, he's here, are you ready?"

The door opened and Abigail walked in behind her. "Yes, here are your sunhat, sunglasses, bottle of water and sunscreen." From behind, a sunhat flopped onto Mildred's head. "And here are your glasses, dear." Which appeared over her shoulder along with a bottle of water and sunscreen, then Abigail donned her own sunhat and glasses.

Mildred leaned toward Ferdinand. "Would you put my things in your pocket, please." She shoved the sunscreen and water at him.

The weight of the water pulled on the lines of his light jacket. "Certainly, Ms. Mildred."

Abby chimed in. "Here's mine too, please," and a water bottle appeared over Mildred's shoulder.

"Certainly, Ms. Abby." He moved the sunscreen to an inside pocket and placed the water in the empty pocket.

"Oh, and here's our room key, Ferdinand." Mildred smiled and tucked it into his handkerchief pocket.

"Are we ready now, ladies?"

Mildred smiled. "Yes, would you be so kind as to walk ahead and hail a taxi. My sister and I will be right behind you."

He turned to scurry away.

She hooked her arm in Abby's. "That rat is going to regret the day he ever met us, and whatever we do, we will not let that slimy eel out of our sight, one of us will have an eye on him at all times. I don't want to give him an opportunity to use your credit card again."

"But Millie, we suspended it."

"I know, but I don't want him to know that, not just yet. I have a plan."

When they reached the stairs, Jeremiah was waiting. "I see the plan is beginning."

Ferdinand stood at the bottom of the stairs with a taxi

door open.

Mildred peered over the rail. "Indeed, Captain Baby. He's in for the ride of his life."

Jeremiah tipped his hat, laughed, reached for her hand and kissed it.

She flashed hot and put her hand to her heart. "Well, that was a most pleasant surprise."

He grinned. "Reel in this fish and I'll kiss you on the cheek too."

Smiling she leaned toward him and said, "When we catch him, I'll arm wrestle you to see who fillets him."

A roar of laughter erupted from the Captain. "Bless your hearts, I love you two. Be careful. Call me if you need me."

"We shall, Captain Baby." She smiled.

Halfway down the stairs, Abigail turned toward Jeremiah and waved. "Goodbye, dear. We'll see you at lunch."

Down the gangway they trotted, at the bottom, they turned to wave again, then into the waiting taxi and off they went.

Mildred leaned forward. "Driver do you know the

Beach Comber Shop?"

"Yes, ma'am."

"That's where I want to go, please."

"Yes, ma'am."

Ferdinand chattered away. "So, you are in the market for a bathing costume, Ms. Mildred?"

"Yes, Abigail has convinced me to try new things and I think I should like to prance up and down a tropical beach in a swimsuit. Did you bring your trunks, Ferdinand?"

His eyebrows rose. "Well, no, I didn't assume that you would actually want to swim."

The taxi stopped at the curb in from of the store.

"Abby, you and I are going shopping? Ferdinand, would you like to join us inside or wait outside?"

"I shall …"

"Whichever you prefer, dear, but stay close, please don't leave us stranded, we wouldn't know what to do without you. Come along, Abby. There is adventure to be pursued." She exited the cab and glanced down the street behind them. "That looks like the man I saw talking to Jeremiah across the room at the dance."

Abigail turned to look. "Who?"

"Never mind, he's going the other way. It must be my imagination."

Inside the shop, Mildred could see Ferdinand watching through the window, the sales lady took a tape measure from around her neck and proceeded to measure each of them. She nodded, walked to a rack on the wall and flipped through the inventory, stopping at a beautiful royal blue suit with a coordinating floral sarong, she handed it to Mildred and directed her to the changing room. Next the girl walked to a different section and again flipped until she stopped on a bright purple, one-shouldered suit, with a short skirt, handed it to Abigail and pointed to the other dressing room.

"Millie, I can't believe we're doing this."

"Why not, Abby, you were the one saying we'd never taken a cruise before, I'm just embracing your idea."

"I know, but a makeover and a new party dress is one thing, being half-naked in public is another."

Mildred laughed. "I'm supposed to be the up-tight

sister. What's wrong?"

Abigail, tapped at her door.

Mildred's door cracked.

"This is what's wrong." Abigail stood there in the most alluring, yet modest swimsuit Mildred had ever seen.

"Dear, take the skirt off and let me see the suit."

She shook her head *no*. "I don't dare."

Don't be ridiculous, I'm your sister."

Abigail squinched her lips, but complied.

"Abby! Who knew you still had a figure. You look wonderful."

She looked down at the suit. "But is this too revealing? I'm embarrassed."

"Honey, if I had your shape, I wouldn't be embarrassed. We *are* taking that suit, get the girl to remove the tags."

Abigail's eyes knit together and the corners of her mouth turned down. "Let me see yours first."

Mildred opened the door and stepped before the full-length mirror. "Oh, my!"

Abigail sucked in a full mouth of air. "Millie, you

look like a plus-sized model, with the emphasis on model, not the plus-sized, I mean and you have an hour-glass shape."

She laughed. "It's this darn suit! It's like that rubber-tube-thing the girls put me in at the dress shop, but I mean it's so comfortable, it feels like a second skin." She pulled the sarong from her waist and looked at her rear. "If I could get rid of some of these ripples in my legs, I wouldn't be half bad."

Abigail looked at the sale's girl and smiled. "We'll take both of these suits."

Mildred added, "And we're wearing them out of here."

The girl beamed. "Yes, ma'am." She rang up the tickets. "That will be four hundred and twenty-five dollars, ma'am."

Abigail's mouth flew open. "Mildred, did you hear the price? Yes, dear, ask Ferdinand to come pay the lady."

"But Millie, it's too much!"

"Just do it, dear. Sashay yourself to the front of the store in that suit, then wave for him to come in."

"Oh, Millie, I can't!"

"Would you rather I sashay my plus-size form in front of the window? Hmmm? And how many other women do you think that oily character has cheated out of that amount of money in one day?"

The sales girl ducked her head and pursed her lips, but said nothing.

Mildred spotted her. "It's okay, dear, we're going to teach him a lesson he won't soon forget. He already owes us over three hundred and forty dollars for dinner, a sailboat tour and a taxi ride."

The girl smiled and nodded.

Abigail stomped her foot and walked to the window. "Oh, alright!" She smiled, turned toward the glass and stood on her tiptoes.

Mildred laughed because she knew Abigail was tiptoeing to give her legs more shape.

"Yoo-hoo, Ferdinand, come here, please."

As he entered the shop, he saw Abigail. "Oh my, how enchanting you look."

Mildred stepped forward.

Ferdinand stopped in his tracks.

She smiled. "What do you think?"

"I'm, I'm in awe. You are both so ..."

Mildred laughed. "What? We're both, what? So well-formed for mature widows?"

He nodded. "Yes," he smiled, "that and so much more."

She turned toward the mirror again and placed the sarong around her waist. "Pay the lady, please, Ferdinand and Abby, you can put on your skirt now."

The girl showed him the amount.

His eyes fluttered a bit.

Mildred turned to him and smiled. "You don't mind, do you, dear?"

"Oh, certainly not, Ms. Mildred. You are both so charming it will be my pleasure."

She laughed. "After all, you can only marry one of us. The other, whoever the unlucky one is, will need to attract another man. Don't you agree?"

For a moment, his face blanched white, like he was going to faint, but he pulled himself together and reached for his wallet. This time he pulled out a green card, paid the bill and took the receipt. "Where to now, ladies?"

Mildred pointed to the window, but looked at the sales girl. "Is that a public beach?"

"Yes, ma'am it is and there's a concession stand to the right, if you need anything," and she winked.

Mildred smiled and nodded. "Let's just walk across the street to the beach. Thank you, dear, you have been most helpful, in fact, I think you deserve a tip. Ferdinand, please give the girl a twenty."

He whipped his head toward the girl, the smile melted from her face. Through clenched teeth he said, "My pleasure."

"Abigail, come dear. Ferdinand will you carry the bag with the clothes we worn in here?"

The sales girl quickly folded them and placed them in a bag, handed it to him and took the twenty.

With a very tight smile, he nodded his head to the sales lady. "Certainly, Ms. Mildred."

Chapter 17

A Beautiful, Sandy Beach

They walked out the door and crossed the street. Stepping onto the sand, Mildred lifted her foot to remove one shoe, then the other. "Please put these in the bag, Ferdinand. I'm going in the water, Abby, would you like to join me?"

"Yes, but let me take off my shoes." She kicked them off and left them at Ferdinand's feet. She hurried toward her sister who dropped her sarong on the creamy-white sand, just above the waterline. "Millie do I have to take off my swim skirt?"

"Not if you don't want to, dear, but honestly, you have nothing to be ashamed of, truly, you look remarkable for a woman of eighty."

"Oh, Millie, you know I'm only sixty-five"

"And a half, dear."

Abigail tightened her fists. "Oh, alright then." She scooted the skirt to her ankles and stepped out of it.

Mildred instructed her. "Now turn, smile and wave at Ferdinand, dear."

True to form she did exactly as Mildred said, except she waved with more enthusiasm than necessary.

Through a smile, but with clenched teeth, Mildred said, "That's good, dear, you can stop now."

Abigail spun toward her. "Millie, you're treating him like a dog."

"Yes, dear." She smiled and gave a queenly wave. "Just like the dog who invited us to dinner last night and put the bill on your credit card."

"Okay, I see your point, but now what're we going to do?"

"We're going to prance around a bit in the water and work up a thirst." She smiled again.

"Then what?"

"Then we're going to be thirsty, but our water is going to be too warm to be satisfying. You can put your skirt on now, Abby, if you would like." She headed out of the water straight toward Ferdinand, picking up her sarong on the way and trailing it behind her across the cool, dry sand.

Abigail noticed a certain twist to Mildred's walk that she'd never noticed before. She hurried to her side. "Millie, have you hurt your knee or something?"

She snapped her head toward her sister. "No! I haven't hurt my knee. Quiet! Now come on." She faced Ferdinand again and her smile returned.

He had procured three chaise lounges and placed them under a stand of palm trees. He stood when they walked up. "Did you enjoy the water?"

Mildred pulled her sarong around her middle. "Yes," she smiled, "did you enjoy the view?"

He laughed. "You are toying with me, Ms. Mildred."

"I never 'toy,' Ferdinand, but I am thirsty. Can you hand me my water bottle?"

"My pleasure." His jacket rested on the back of the center chair. He reached in each pocket and retrieved the plastic bottles. "For you, mademoiselle," then one to Abigail.

Mildred tipped her bottle and a long, slow swallow slid down her throat. "Oh, my goodness, wet, but not very refreshing, it has no chill left. Can we get something cooler?" She glanced around and spotted the concession stand the sales girl had mentioned. "Will you come with me and help me choose a refreshing tropical drink, Ferdinand?"

"It would be my pleasure and, Ms. Abby, would you like to join us or remain here to guard our most favored seats."

Mildred's eyes cut toward the chairs.

Abigail smiled, tipped her head back and donned her sunhat and glasses. "Oh, I shall stay here to protect what you've provided, but please bring me a fruity drink with a tiny umbrella, I've always wanted one of those."

Mildred strolled ahead, but he caught up with her and grinned. "May I recommend a fruity beverage that I've had many times? It's called a Sunrise. It contains crushed ice, so it's very refreshing and pieces of fruit with an umbrella, as your sister requested."

They arrived at a tiki-type bar, with its thatched roof and bamboo skirting.

Mildred leaned her elbows on the rail. "Sounds marvelous, dear."

Ferdinand ordered. "Waiter, may we have three Sunrises?"

"Yes sir, coming right up." A blender whizzed, ice smashed against the sides, then was added to three large bellied glasses. The waiter added chopped pineapple, cherries and something she didn't recognize on top of the ice. A shaker of liquid was poured over it all, forcing the fruit into a swirl with the ice. Finally, a toothpick with a small umbrella on top was jabbed into the mixture, along with a skinny straw. "That will be forty-eight dollars, sir."

The wallet was produced and as she watched, he placed the green card into the hand of the waiter.

"Thank you, sir." The waiter rang it up. "Here's your receipt."

Mildred didn't have the heart to demand a tip for the guy, so she took her drink and placed the icy glass to her cheek. She removed the umbrella and slid the rim of the glass to her mouth, but Ferdinand couldn't see that no liquid passed her lips. "Oh, this is marvelous. Just what the day required."

She held his arm as they strolled back to their beach chairs.

When they arrived, Ferdinand handed Abigail her glass.

Mildred tried to get her attention, but failed.

Abigail, who was seated on the furthest chaise, eagerly took the glass and sipped in a large mouth-full of the mixture. "Oh, this is wonderful, so sweet, so fruity," she looked up and smiled, "so tropical. What's that unusual taste? I can't seem to identify it."

"I'm sure you are referring to the passion fruit, dear lady."

"Hmmm, Yum!"

Mildred rolled her eyes, but it escaped Abigail's notice.

Ferdinand seated himself on the center chair and scooted back, to rest against the slightly reclined slats.

Mildred parked herself on the chair closest to the bar, pretended to take a sip, then spilled a little splash into the sand. "Oh, how refreshing! You're right, Abby, this is powerfully good stuff." She cut her eyes toward her sister who sipped-away, oblivious of the warning. "You're a marvel, Ferdinand, so knowledgeable. Yum!" Another splash was gobbled up by the sand.

A sucking noise from the straw indicated Ferdinand had reached the bottom of his glass.

Mildred glanced at him. "I think we have time for another one or two of these before we need to return to the ship." Another splash hit the sand, then Mildred whispered, "Ferdinand, do you think we should have another? Just say no, if you think we shouldn't."

"I'm sure it would be fine to have another, Ms. Mildred."

She continued to whisper, "Oh dear, it looks like my sister is napping. Please take her glass, so it doesn't spill on her beautiful new swim skirt, Ferdinand."

He whispered in return. "My pleasure, madam," and reached for the drink, "do you think she would mind if I finished hers?"

"I'm sure she wouldn't mind and look, mine is gone too," she giggled. "Where's that waiter?"

She hoisted her glass in the air, "Yoo-hoo, waiter," he hurried over. She handed him her glass, then reached for Abby's and Ferdinand's. Slurring her words, a little she said. "Two more please."

"Very good, madam, and may I take the gentleman's card to save time?"

She stuck her hand his direction. "The waiter would like your Visa, dear."

With no hesitation, he pulled the green card from his wallet and handed it to her.

She passed it to the man, who quickly returned to the bar. She touched Ferdinand's arm. "Let's not disturb Abby, she may still be resting up from that reaction to the Newberg sauce."

"You are such a good sister, Ms. Mildred."

"Thank you, oh look, here are our drinks. I've never had one of these before today, but I think I could drink them till *sunrise*, get it?" She giggled. "Drink Sunrises, till sunrise."

He chuckled. "Yes, they are delicious and so relaxing." He slurped away with gusto.

Mildred continued to slosh small amounts of her drink into the sand. "Tell me about your acquisition business, Ferdi," she giggled, "can I call you Ferdi? Or would that be too forward of me?"

"Certainly, dear lady. I would be honored for you to call me that."

She hoisted her glass in the air and the waiter came running. "Two more, please." She handed him the card she hadn't returned to Ferdinand.

"Tell me about your business travels, Ferdi. Where've you been?"

Chapter 18

Very Talkative

"I was most recently in Marrakesh, Morocco."

"Oh my, how exotic!"

He slurped down the third drink and she handed him hers.

"What were you acquiring in Morocco?"

He snickered. "I was courting a wealthy heiress who had a beautiful yacht, the *Amelia Rose*. She had asked me to travel to Greece with her. I agreed of course," he snickered again, "but while she was ashore shopping, I told the captain that she was aboard and she wished to set sail immediately."

Mildred leaned closer. "And did he?"

"But of course, whatever Amelia wanted, she got."

He laughed without reserve.

"What happened to Amelia, Ferdi?"

"Oh, she probably called her daddy, to come for her?"

"What happened to the yacht?"

He waved his free hand in the air. "I had telephoned some merchants that I do business with and they picked it up as soon as we left Marrakesh."

"What happened to the crew?"

"Oh, Ms. Mildred, we are not murderers, oh no, when the yacht was out at sea, they were sent back to Morocco by life boat."

"That's wonderful Ferdi. You've had such an exciting life. Tell me about your favorite acquisition."

"Ahhh, yes, my favorite piece was a Van Gogh."

Mildred's forehead wrinkled and she drew her head back. "You mean Vincent Van Gogh the painter?"

"Yes, in 2002, some men broke into the Amsterdam Van Gogh Museum and stole his famous work, 'View of the Sea at Scheveningen.'"

"Ferdi, *you* broke into a museum?"

"No, no, no. I *acquired* the painting from one of the

men who stole it," he chuckled heartily, "when he wasn't looking."

She leaned to his shoulder. "It must be very valuable."

"At the time, it was worth about fifteen million dollars. I may have to sell it one day to finance my business."

"Oh, Ferdi, how exciting. What happened to the painting?"

Laughing again, he crammed his hand into his glass to fish-out some fruit. "It is hanging in the bathroom of my flat in London."

Her shoulders shot back. "Your bathroom?"

"Yes, the colors look superb against my steel gray walls and stainless-steel fixtures."

She composed herself and snuggled in close to his shoulder. "What other acquisitions do you have?"

"Oh, not many? A few gold coins, a Ming vase, and a few other trifles. Most must eventually be sold to pay for the next venture." He started to nod off to sleep.

Mildred took the glass from his hand and waved for the waiter, who rushed to her side. "My friends seem to have had too much fun today. Could you hail a taxi for me and help to get them in, we will return to the Princess of the Sea."

The waiter whistled and waved for assistance.

A cabbie ran across the sand to help.

Mildred pulled two twenties from Ferdinand's wallet, giving one to the waiter who smiled and tipped his head. "Thank you, madam."

The other she handed to the taxi driver. "This should be enough to get us to the pier and perhaps help me get," she cleared her throat, "the gentleman and lady up the stairs."

"Yes, ma'am."

The waiter and driver lifted Ferdinand between them, Mildred tossed his jacket across one of his shoulders and they shuffled him to the cab.

Mildred scooped up the bag of clothes and went to her sister, by that time the waiter had returned to assist her. He placed one of Abigail's arms over his shoulder, Mildred did the same on the other side. "Come on, Abby, let's get you back."

On the drive, Mildred phoned with an update, "I might need some help when we arrive, Jeremiah. We should be there in five minutes."

When they reached the ship, he stood at the top of the gangway and sent two staff members to the taxi to help with Mr. Modesto, while Mildred and the driver got Abigail aboard. Jeremiah smiled. "Looks like you had an eventful morning and I totally approve of the swimwear."

"Stop it, Captain Baby." One of Mildred's shoulders bore Abigail's weight. "Jeremiah, will you do whatever you wish with Mr. Greasy, but if you could provide me a rolling deck chair, I'll get my sister back to our room."

He directed the two staffers. "Gentlemen, escort Mr. Modesto to the infirmary, I don't think he should be left alone."

The two dragged him across the deck, with his arms over their shoulders, one holding his jacket and one gripping his belt in the back.

"As for Ms. Abigail, we can do better than a deck chair." He lifted her free arm and placed it around his shoulders, then placed his other arm behind her knees. Her head flopped onto his chest. "Come now, Ms. Abigail, let's get you to your stateroom."

Mildred took her sister's other arm, laid it on her body, so it wouldn't dangle and followed Jeremiah closely. "Oh Jeremiah, what a mess. I don't have our key, it was in Ferdinand's jacket."

"Not a problem." He lifted his hand that was behind Abigail's knees and mashed an intercom button in the hallway. "This is Captain Williams, I need a porter with a master key at this location."

Almost immediately Isaac rushed to his assistance.

Mildred smiled at him. "Thank you ever so much, Isaac."

He plopped the master key on the pad and turned the handle.

The Captain faced him. "That will be all."

Isaac nodded. "Yes, Sir," and backed away.

Pushing the door wide, Mildred rushed to the bed and pulled the covers back. "Just place her here, Jeremiah."

He gently positioned Abigail's body. "I'll allow you to do the rest, Millie."

She placed her hand on his arm. "Thank you, Jeremiah, allow me time to change clothes and leave a note for Abby, in case she wakes up while I'm gone, then can you meet me in the dining room? I have a lot to tell you."

Chapter 19

Much to Discuss

Moments later, Mildred entered the dining hall.

The Captain was waiting. "Millie, I've poured you some tea and I have a table, please take your time and choose what you'd like to eat."

They both chose several delicacies, then walked to the table Jeremiah indicated.

He pulled out her chair and seated her, by the time he reached his seat, she had drunk half of her tea.

Jeremiah beckoned a waiter. "A fresh glass of sweet tea for Ms. Butterfly, please," then he turned to her. "Are you okay?"

"Yes, yes, I'm fine, but our outing this morning has

left me a little thirsty."

The waiter delivered another glass of tea, which she slowly sipped.

Jeremiah nodded. "Ahhh, I noticed the snazzy, new swim suits."

She chuckled and leaned forward. "We stuck, Ferdinand, with the bill, over four hundred dollars, but I didn't have much to drink, so I'm parched."

The Captain laughed. "Well I can see that Mr. Modesto did, but I'm shocked about Ms. Abigail."

"Don't blame her, dear. She didn't know it was *loaded,* she thought it was fruit punch and I couldn't warn her without tipping off that greasy eel. Of course, he chose the drink, a quart in each glass, a Sunrise, I think it was called."

Jeremiah placed his hand over his mouth. "Oh, my, those are potent."

"Well, Abby only drank a half. I slowly poured my first one out into the sand. Greasy drank his, then finished-off Abby's. I gave him a chance to call it quits, but he said it would be okay to have another, so I ordered two more to loosen his tongue. It goes without saying, my second one was also gobbled up by the sand, but by the third round, he drank his and mine too."

The Captain frowned. "So, if I've counted correctly, that was four Sunrises for Mr. Modesto?"

Mildred frowned. "Plus, he finished Abby's and jammed his hand into all the glasses to get the liquor saturated fruit."

He covered his mouth to keep from laughing. "So, did it work, loosening his tongue, I mean?"

"Yes, until he passed out after number four and a half."

Jeremiah leaned in. "What did you learn, Millie? Is this man a gigolo?"

She reached toward him and whispered. "That and more. He's a swindler, a con man, an art thief, though I must say, the Van Gogh he stole had already been stolen and he stole it from the original thieves, so I'm not sure how much that counts, but he still has it."

"At the very least he's in possession of stolen good valued in the millions."

She patted his arm. "He even stole a yacht."

"What?"

"From an heiress while she was shopping, but he made it clear that the crew were sent back to Marrakesh, unharmed."

"Millie, we need to get Interpol involved, they're the International Criminal Police."

"Okay, but can we have one more dinner with him before they bust him? I have a plan."

Jeremiah laughed and whispered, "Just one more dinner, or I'll have to have you and Ms. Abigail arrested as con-artists."

She laughed and patted his arm again. "Deal! Now let's eat, I'm starved."

Chapter 20

Awake

Abigail sat up with a groan and stretched. "Oh, my, I have a headache." Her hand swept to her forehead. "What time is it?"

"It's three in the afternoon, sweetie."

"Three o'clock, what am I doing in bed?" She looked down. "And why am I still in my bathing suit."

"You've had quite a day." Mildred laughed. "Think, Abby, what's the last thing you remember?"

"Well we bought swimsuits, then we went to the beach and walked in the water. Then," she paused, "the rest is a little fuzzy."

"Okay, do you remember wanting a fruity drink?"

"Hmmm, Yes, I do, oh, it was delicious."

"And it was also *fully leaded,* Abby."

"You mean with alcohol?"

"Yes, and with only a half a glass, you were out like a light."

"How did I get back here and into bed?"

Mildred laughed again. "Well the story includes a waiter, a taxi driver and Jeremiah."

She threw her hands over her face. "Oh no! Not the Captain!"

"He carried you to the room like you were a lifeless twig, dear."

"No, stop it!" She looked up and frowned. "What do you mean like a lifeless twig?"

"Oh, don't worry, I told him you didn't know it was loaded. He was very sweet and understanding."

Abigail hung her head. "I can never face him again." She suddenly remembered. "What about Ferdinand?"

Mildred chuckled. "You mean, Ferdi? We got pretty chummy while you were out."

"Stop it. What happened to him?"

"After drinking four Sunrises and the other half of

yours, he passed out, but before he did, I found out lots of dirt on him and he's now under the doctor's watchful eye in the infirmary."

"Will he be okay?" Her eyebrows knit together and her tone shifted. "What dirt?"

"He'll be fine, except for a major headache tomorrow."

"I found out that he's more than a gigolo, he a crook," she leaned forward, "—a criminal—a thief. He has stolen items, worth millions, in his apartment in London." Mildred stood. "Let me get you something for your headache." Taking a bottle from the nightstand, she dashed out two pills and handed them to Abigail along with a bottle of water. "Here, take these and prop-up on our pillows for a little while and I'll explain."

The next half hour Mildred spent detailing all of Ferdinand's exploits.

"Now Abby, I think we need to shower, go get our hair styled, then get some food in you."

Chapter 21

Scuttlebutt

Mildred and Abigail sat in the salon chairs.

Shell smiled at the reflections in the mirror. "Well ladies, the scuttlebutt says, that you've had an exciting day."

Abigail frowned. "What the heck is scuttlebutt and who told you that we've had an exciting day?"

Becca grinned. "Scuttlebutt is the ship's gossip. You know, people tell hairdressers everything."

Abigail frowned again. "That's not nice, you shouldn't gossip."

Becca leaned forward and placed her hands on Abigail's shoulders. "Oh, Ms. Abby, we were only teasing. We're sorry."

Shell smiled and said, "Let's get down to business. What do you need for tonight?"

Mildred responded. "Something simple this time, girls, suitable for dinner at the Captain's table."

Shell asked, "And what are you wearing tonight?"

But Abigail smiled and replied, "Our LBDs, dear. You know every girl needs a little black dress."

"Yes ma'am, that's so true. Two simple, but elegant hairdos and face-paint, coming right up."

Chapter 22

I Don't Think I Can

In stylish black dresses, their hair nicely done and light makeup applied, they entered the dining hall.

"Oh, Millie, I don't think I can face sitting at Jeremiah's table tonight."

"Don't be silly, Abby, he will hardly recognize you, now that you are conscious, fully clothed and you're not drooling."

She stomped her foot. "Millie! That does it, I'm going to eat in our cabin."

A warm, sympathetic voice drifted over their shoulders. "No need to do that, Ms. Abigail, your sister explained what happened, I think no less of you. Now let's go have a nice dinner."

Abigail turned around with tear-filled eyes. "Oh, Jeremiah, I'm so embarrassed."

He placed his hand on her shoulder, leaned close and smiled. "There's no need for that. It was all in the line of duty."

Mildred echoed him. "Yes, all in the line of duty, dear and you were brilliant. Here's a hanky, now blot, don't wipe." She handed her a tissue and smiled. "We have one more part of the plan to execute and it will be complete. The captain knows the whole story."

Following dinner, Abigail scanned the room for Ferdinand, but he was nowhere to be seen.

"Don't fret, Abby, he's probably still sleeping it off in the infirmary, but we can go by to be sure."

True to her word, they stopped and asked after Mr. Modesto's condition.

The doctor smiled. "He'll be fine, ladies. He just had way too much alcohol and he's sleeping, but I'll have someone monitor his vital signs regularly through the night. Over the years, I've seen more than a few who've *over-celebrated*, shall we say, but it's charming of you to look in on his condition. And Ms. Fine, may I say you look very elegant this evening."

She lifted her shoulders and stared into his eyes. "Why thank you, Dr. Fielding. How kind of you to say."

Mildred took her by the elbow. "Okay, Abby, now that we have been assured of Ferdinand's welfare, we need to go get some rest ourselves. I'm sure we will see him tomorrow. Doctor, when he wakes up, would you please tell him that we checked on him?"

He dipped his head. "Certainly Ms. Butterfly, that will be no problem at all."

Mildred gently grasped her sister's elbow. "Come, dear, let's go. We have plans to make."

Back in their stateroom, Abigail lamented. "Poor Ferdinand, he's still out cold."

Mildred fumed. "Poor Ferdinand, my foot! He chose the drinks and intended to do to us exactly what he did to himself. He's the blackguard here, not us."

"Oh, I'm sorry, I just feel guilty."

"Guilty about what, Abby? Drinking half of the beverage he chose for you that was loaded with alcohol and him knowing that we didn't drink, then you passing out from drinking too much of the drink he chose, or for him being a glutton and drinking four and a half Sunrises? What part do you feel guilty about?"

"Well, when you put it that way."

"That's the only way it can be *put*, Abby. Now stop being so soft, that man's a snake and we're going to catch him in his own net."

Abigail frowned. "You mixed your metaphors, dear."

Mildred growled, *Grrrr!* "Abigail!"

Chapter 23

Part Two of the Plan

After breakfast the next day, about mid-morning, Mildred declared, "Okay, Abby, I've prayed about it and this is what I think we're to do. As soon as we see Ferdinand, we'll go to him and act all sympathetic and apologetic or," she frowned, "at least I'll let you do that part."

"Okay, but what do we say if he asks how we got back to the ship?"

"Just say something like, 'Oh my goodness, I don't know how you managed, we were both in such a state,' and that's true. You were passed out and I was furious with him, so we were both in *such a state*, alright? So, you don't have to lie."

"Thank you, Millie, you're so good to me."

Mildred rolled her eyes. "My pleasure Abby, now let's head to the dining room for lunch. We may have to wait awhile."

But—*tap, tap, tap.*

Mildred opened the door, instantly putting on a smile. "Oh, Ferdi, it's you, darling."

One hand leaned against the door frame, his normally erect posture sagged in the shoulders, tired eyes, decorated by tiny red lines, stared at Mildred. "I wanted to see if you ladies were okay."

Mildred's face lost its smile. "We're fine, how are you, dear? You look dreadful."

He dropped his hand from the doorjamb and tried to straighten his posture. "I'm okay, Ms. Mildred."

"Now Ferdi, darling," her smile returned, "after yesterday, please call me Millie. From now on, we only use our formal names on our wedding invitations."

"Wedding," he gulped, "invitations?"

"Yes, dear, now let's go get some lunch, afterwards Abby and I want to get our hair done and shop again before our celebration this evening at the Savoy. I want to look my best for," she pinched his cheek, "my sweetums."

In a daze, she spun him around. "Abby, come on, we have a lot to do today and close the door behind you, please."

Entering the dining hall, Mildred spotted Jeremiah and waved. "Yoo-hoo, Captain, we have some good news for you."

He strolled up. "What good news would that be, Ms. Butterfly?"

"We," she tugged on Ferdinand's arm, "we're going to the Savoy again tonight to celebrate."

The Captain folded his arms. "What are you celebrating?"

"Well, Captain, you may soon be called upon to perform a ceremony." She placed her index finger at her lips and grinned. "That's all I can say for now."

"May I be the first to congratu …"

"Shhh, shhh, no, no Captain, we don't want to jinx it, now do we?" She giggled.

The Captain smiled. "Certainly, I understand, now if you'll excuse me, please enjoy your lunch."

"Ferdi, dearest, would you get our drinks and this time," she winked, "I'll fix you a plate."

He wandered toward the drinks isle.

Abigail turned to her sister. "What happened to the sympathetic blah-blah-blah?"

"I didn't count on him showing up at our door without calling first, now did I?" Mildred knit her eyebrows together. "I had to improvise. I just said the first thing that came into my head." Then she smiled at her sister. "Good thing I prayed, huh?"

"You were always quick on your feet, I'll give you that Millie, and you've always had a good head on your shoulders."

"Thank you, Abby, you've always had a head on your shoulders too."

Abigail smiled, then she frowned. "Millie, that's not nice."

Mildred laughed. "Remember, you're the nice one and you always have been, now quiet," she smiled, "here comes Ferdinand."

"I've placed our drinks on a table, ladies."

Mildred handed him a plate with a dinner roll on it.

"I'll need to learn all of your favorite foods if I'm to be a good ..." she placed her fingers to her lips again, giggled and lifted her shoulders, "you know."

After filling their plates, they moved to the table Ferdinand had secured.

Turning to her sister, Mildred chatted. "Abby, do you think my wedding dress should be white or off-white, since I've been married before?"

"You look so much better in white, you know you're a vivid person. I think off-white would spoil the whole look."

"Hmm, I agree, or should I go for a non-traditional red?"

Abigail pondered for a moment, then turned to Ferdinand. "What do you think?"

"I'm sorry ladies, I think I'm still a little mentally flushed from the sun and too much to drink. I need to go rest before we go to the dinner this evening."

Mildred cooed, "Oh certainly, Ferdi, you get some rest and pick us up at six. I've made a reservation." She grinned.

He stood, bowed slightly and said, "If you will excuse me."

As he walked away, Mildred fought hard not to laugh out loud. She spotted the Captain. "Pssst! Jeremiah, pssst!"

The Captain approached and smiled. "How's it going?"

"Fine, but you'd better alert the watchman at the gangway that Ferdinand may try to do a runner. I've made reservations at the Savoy for tonight and we'll spring our trap then, just don't let that slippery eel squirm his way off of this ship and have your brig ready for tonight. You can call the local authorities and have them on stand-by for about eight to respond to the Savoy, a fraudster will need to be picked up."

Jeremiah laughed then whispered. "Maybe I'll wait for the call from the restaurant before I call the police, otherwise, it could be considered entrapment."

Mildred chuckled and winked. "Good point, Captain Baby, now, Abby, we need to get some rest."

Chapter 24

Runner

They arrived at their stateroom and were preparing for a nap, when the phone rang.

Abigail answered. "Hello, hello."

"Who is it, Abby?"

Abigail put her hand over the receiver. "Well, I can hear Jeremiah's voice, but he's not talking into the mouthpiece."

Mildred tilted her head toward the receiver and whispered, "Listen! It sounds like he's talking to Ferdinand."

They both pressed their heads to the phone.

"Yes, Mr. Modesto, we have a very fine menswear shop aboard. I'm sure you can find a suitable dress shirt for this evening. What you'll find ashore will mostly be casual wear. — Yes, we also have an ATM in the lounge, so you can replenish your cash. — Flowers for the ladies, yes, the shop behind the rotunda will have an ample supply, so you see, there's no need to waste a trip ashore. — Please enjoy your afternoon, sir."

There was a momentary pause, followed by Jeremiah's laughter into the speaker.

"Did, you ladies, catch that? You were right again. I think he was trying to do a runner."

Mildred gushed. "You were splendid, Jeremiah. Thank you again for all of your help. Who knew when we came aboard that we would be immersed in a such intrigues?" She laughed heartily.

Jeremiah chuckled. "Yes, who knew indeed?"

"Goodbye, dear." She hung up the phone.

"Now, Abby, for a nap."

Chapter 25

The Objective

After their nap and a shower, Shell and Becca greeted them in the salon.

Shell grinned and asked, "What's our objective for tonight Ms. Mildred and Ms. Abigail?"

Mildred squinted. "Our objective? Who've you girls been talking to?"

Shell looked over at Becca. "I was just kidding around. I didn't mean anything by it."

Mildred looked at Abigail, then back at them. "Okay, but you girls always seem to be two steps ahead of us."

"We're not, you just always seem to be on a mission when you come in here, so I thought you might be tonight."

"As a matter of fact, we are. We have a dinner," she emphasized the word, "*engagement.*" Mildred looked at Abigail and smiled. "Make me up to look like a Jezebel and fix my sister up like Mata Hari."

Becca and Shell looked at each other and back at Mildred

Shell suggested, "Why don't you let us make you up to look-like lovely rich ladies, instead?"

"Very well," Mildred laughed, "if you insist."

The girls set to work with their usual fervor.

An hour later, the chairs turned toward their mirrors.

Mildred's hair was swept up in a fabulous twist in the back. The front and sides were teased and sprayed in soft flips blown back, away from her face. Her makeup was barely visible, yet her cheeks, eyes, and lips shimmered. "Well, I've never."

Shell laughed and leaned down to her shoulder. "Never what, Ms. M.?"

"I've never known anyone as talented as you girls."

Abigail eyed Mildred's reflection. "Millie, you look so sophisticated and so lovely."

Mildred diverted her eyes to Abigail's mirror. "Oh, Abby, honey, if your hair were darker, you'd look just like you did as the Homecoming Queen your senior year.

Her teased hair was slightly high at the crown and smoothed, but not like helmet-hair, it was softly brushed into a beautiful Pixie-do with wisps along the sides, curled toward her face. "I can't believe how young they've made us look." She started to tear up.

"Abigail, don't you cry, you'll ruin your makeup."

Becca handed her a tissue and three voices erupted. "Blot, don't wipe."

Shell looked into the mirrors. "Next stop, dress shop."

Abigail turned to her sister. "Do we really need more new clothes?"

"Yes, Abby, we do, just relax and enjoy the ride. Okay girls, let's go see what you have in mind for tonight."

Chapter 26

Pants or a Dress

Shell held up a pantsuit in an icy blue, soft chiffon fabric and a long, slinky white dress. "Tonight, you have a choice, Ms. M. Which will it be?"

She plopped her hands to her cheeks. "I don't know, Shell, I can't imagine myself in either one."

Abigail giggled. "Save the long white dress for her next wedding," and she grinned at Mildred. "Put her in the chiffon pantsuit for tonight."

Shell nodded. "I think I agree, chiffon for tonight."

Becca gave Abigail two choices. "Okay Ms. Fine, which will it be for you tonight? This candy apple red pantsuit or this soft sky-blue dress?"

"Going with the theme here, I'll save the blue dress

for my Maid of Honor dress for Millie's next wedding," she winked at Mildred, "give me the fiery red pants suit."

"Excellent choice." Becca nodded. "Now into the dressing rooms. You have a date to get to."

They emerged from their respective dressing rooms, decked-out to the nines.

Shell pushed a flat box toward Mildred. "Here Ms. M. a necklace to complement your outfit, suited for the richest lady on the ship."

Mildred looked at the lovely necklace, then to Shell. "You do know, don't you, that I'm not rich, right?"

"This will be a loan, from the ship, just for tonight. How does that sound?"

"What if I lose it?"

Laughing, Shell said, "You won't, but if you do, it's insured."

"Very well, in that case." Mildred slipped the necklace from its case and slid it around her neck. Can you help me, Shell? What kind of stone is this?"

Shell stood behind her and took the clasp in her hands. "It's a sky-blue topaz."

Mildred looked in the mirror. "Just enough color in the necklace, but it doesn't overwhelm the suit. I like it."

"Me too," said Abigail, as she stepped out in her luxurious red attire.

Becca nodded. "You are both now resplendent. We'll take care of returning your clothes to your cabins."

Mildred waved her hand. "No need dear, we are being called for at our cabin."

"Yes, ma'am. Have fun."

Chapter 27

The Trap

The usual three light taps, drew Abigail's attention. "He's here, Millie." She opened the door with a smile. "Good evening, Ferdinand, you look handsome."

He grinned. "And may I say that you are as charming as ever."

From the bathroom, Mildred emerged.

His eyes scanned her. "And you, Millie, you are exceptionally lovely this evening."

She spun so he could see all sides. "Thank you, Ferdi dearest, we're ready for the Savoy."

He tipped his head and pushed his hand into the hallway. "I will go ahead and be sure our taxi is waiting."

He dashed down the corridor.

As soon as he rounded the corner, "Okay, this is it, Abby, we spring the trap after dinner. Are you ready?"

"But what are we going to do?"

Mildred ushered her toward the gangway. "You just be your charming self, you do that so well, dear."

At the head of the stairs, the Captain waited.

Ferdinand was on the pier.

Mildred smiled and nodded. "The rat will be cornered tonight."

"You call me as soon as you are ready."

"I will, Jeremiah, thank you."

She and Abigail strolled down the stairs. At the bottom, they turned and waved before entering the taxi, with Mildred entering first and sliding to the middle.

Ferdinand proudly announced, "These lovely ladies and I would like to go to the Savoy, please driver."

Mildred hooked her arm in his and chattered away. "Oh, Ferdi, we have so many plans to make before the," she whispered, "you know."

"Yes, I suppose we do," Ferdinand smiled at her,

"unless you would like to postpone until we get home, to include your friends and family."

Mildred patted his arm. "How thoughtful of you, but I'd rather make it official sooner. We can throw a big shebang of a party later and invite all of our friends."

The car pulled up outside the Savoy. The doorman opened the rear passenger door, Ferdinand stepped out. The passenger window lowered and the driver called out the price. Without hesitation, money changed hands. Ferdinand reached for Mildred's hand as the doorman went around to open the door for Abigail.

"Thank you, Ferdi, you are such a gentleman." She grinned at him and cast a glance toward her sister.

Inside the restaurant Mildred address the maître d'. "Reservations for an engagement party, please, under the name of Modesto."

He scanned his list. "Yes, of course, your usual table, madam," and led them to the same table as before. Enjoy your evening." He pulled the chair for Abigail as Ferdinand did the same for Mildred.

She tipped her head and smiled. "How can we not, sir?"

The musician came to the table, but Ferdinand swished his hand. The guitarist nodded and backed away. "Ladies, may I suggest some champagne to toast our celebration?"

Mildred hadn't anticipated this, so paused for a moment and silently prayed, then announced. "No, I think tonight calls for sober-minded reflection. It was only a few days ago that we didn't know each other, now, darling Ferdi, we are preparing for the rest of our lives. That is enough to spin my head without imbibing alcohol." She tilted her head to the side with a delighted smile.

"Yes, I see what you mean. Shall we order and dear sister-to-be Abigail, may I suggest a simpler dish with no wine?"

She smiled and nodded. "Yes, please, what would you recommend."

"Perhaps the grilled lobster tail and we'll have the waiter wrestle it from the shell for you."

She glanced at the menu. "But that is the most expensive dish!"

Mildred turned to her. "This is a party, dear, I think

we should all three have the same."

Ferdinand lifted the menu and gestured. "Excellent, Millie, I approve."

The waiter rushed over.

Mildred allowed Ferdinand to take the lead.

"Three of your very best grilled lobster tails, three salads, three sweet teas and a basket of your fresh bread, s'il vous plait."

The waiter grinned. "Indeed, sir, right away."

Mildred stroked Ferdinand's hand. "Your French is impeccable, darling."

"When love is in the air," he swished his hand with a flourish, "French must be spoken."

She giggled in a girlish manner.

Even Abigail knit her eyebrows and fired off a glance at her. She leaned toward her sister and whispered, "Is that the way I sound, Millie?"

"Shush dear, the music is enchanting."

The waiter arrived with the salads and bread.

Ferdinand took the loaf and napkin, as before, and broke it, offering pieces to Mildred first, then to Abigail."

The waiter returned with plates stacked, each with a large lobster tail, dishes of butter and lemon wedges.

As he served each person, Ferdinand asked, would you assist the ladies with removing the meat from their shells?"

"It will be my pleasure, sir." He started with Abigail's dish. With one scoop of a knife and fork working together, the tail was removed and the shell was placed on an empty plate. Stepping to Mildred's side, he performed the same maneuver. "Sir, may I assist you, it would be a shame to soil such a handsome tuxedo."

"Certainly, and thank you."

The chore was accomplished in seconds.

Ferdinand nodded to him, then to the ladies. "Bon appetit."

Most of the remaining conversation consisted of *oh my, how delicious,* and similar accolades, but, near the end of the meal, Mildred managed to start a discussion of wedding details. "Ferdi, do you wish for the Captain to perform our ceremony or would you prefer a local official handle the details here on the island?"

"Oh, my gracious, Millie, men are not good at such matters, that is better left to the women, do you not agree?" followed by a seemingly genuinely deferential smile.

She cut her eyes coyly at him. "You are so wise, dear, then may I ask what details you have planned for the honeymoon?"

He cleared his throat and blotted the corners of his mouth with his napkin. "Shall we take a stroll on the beach and iron-out the details, Millie? Perhaps you and sister Abigail would like to refresh yourselves in the ladies' room before we go." He stood and put his hand on the back of her chair.

"Yes, we should, Abigail, join me, please." She pushed her chair back. "We'll only be a moment."

They walked toward the restrooms as Ferdinand motioned for the waiter.

Once again, Mildred jerked Abigail behind the potted plant. "Let's see what happens now."

Abigail pushed a large leaf to the side to give her a clear view.

As Mildred suspected, the gold Visa card was

produced from his pocket with a smile and handed to the waiter.

Less than a minute later the waiter reappeared, though they could not hear the conversation, it was clear that the card had been declined. Ferdinand reached for his wallet, but only one twenty-dollar bill remained, presumably for the taxi ride back to the ship.

Mildred motioned to Abigail. "Okay dear, we're on again." She strutted toward the table followed by her sister.

The waiter was standing at attention beside Ferdinand.

"Millie, my darling, there seems to be a problem."

"Yes, Ferdi, what's that?"

"I seem to have forgotten my wallet again and I even tried Ms. Abby's Visa card, but regrettably, it was declined."

Mildred sat up straight. "Oh Abby, there's your card," and plucked it from his hand. "She was afraid she had lost it and called to have the account frozen."

Ferdinand grinned. "Dear, could you pay this poor man who has served us so faithfully tonight?"

Her eyes widened and her mouth dropped, as though surprised. "But Ferdi, neither of us brought our purses."

The waiter used two fingers to wave for someone.

The manager arrived very apologetic. "Forgive me ladies, but there is a problem."

Mildred frowned. "Yes, I know, but perhaps you could call our ship and ask for Captain Williams. I'm sure he will know what to do."

The manager tipped his head, returned to his station, picked up a phone and dialed, while the waiter stood watch beside them.

Mildred sighed and drummed her fingers on the table's edge. "I'm sure our Captain will take care of everything," she smiled at Ferdinand.

Only minutes later, two local Caribbean Police Officers entered the premises.

The manager showed them to the table. "Mr. Modesto, these fine gentlemen will escort you."

"But where to? Why? It's only a small dinner bill."

One officer took him by the elbow and lifted.

Ferdinand glanced at Mildred. "What about the ladies?"

The manager smiled. "Please don't trouble yourself about them, the Captain is coming to escort them back to the ship."

His mouth hung open. "But, but ..."

The second officer stated. "Ferdinand Modesto, you are under arrest for fraud, theft, and possession of stolen goods in excess of fifteen million dollars."

"What? How'd you? — Millie!"

Her eyes twinkled and she grinned. "Oh, please, Ferdi, call me Princess Butterfly."

The officers led him through the restaurant for all to see.

Captain Williams held the door as the police pushed him toward a patrol car, then Jeremiah strolled to the table. "Ladies, excellent work."

The manager arrived at his side, Jeremiah turned and handed him a check. "I'm sure this will cover the cost of the dinner, a nice tip for the server and a little extra for your inconvenience."

The manager looked at the check, smiled and offered his hand to Jeremiah. "You are a true gentleman, Captain," then nodded. "Thank you."

Jeremiah placed his hand on Mildred's chair. "Shall we go ladies?"

The waiter assisted Abigail and they joined the Captain as he walked casually toward the door.

Abigail turned. "Jeremiah, you're absolutely splendid."

"Thank you, Ms. Abby, but it's you two wonderful ladies who are splendid."

The doorman whistled for a taxi that arrived immediately.

Jeremiah continued the conversation as they rode. "I have notified Interpol that two famous, yet unassuming detectives have captured a criminal wanted in several countries."

Mildred stared at him. "Detectives?"

His face dropped its smile. "Why, yes, the ladies of the Fine~Butterfly Detective Agency."

Mildred roared with laughter. "But Jeremiah, we're not detectives! That was our husbands' business, Henry Fine and Maxwell Butterfly."

His eyes widened. "But it sounds so ... feminine."

"Doesn't it though?" And she laughed again. "In the

early days of their work, they got lots of teasing about that, but as word of their success spread, one guy suggested they change the name to the Exceptional~Lepidoptera Detective Agency. Yep, that would make Abby, Abigail Exceptional, her name sounds 'fine,' but as for me, I'd be, Mildred Lepidoptera, it makes me sound like a dinosaur hunter." She laughed again.

Abigail inserted, "I wouldn't mind being known as exceptional," and beamed.

The Captain laughed. "Well, I think you two girls should take-up the family business. You're ..."

Mildred leaned to see her sister's face. "Abby, perhaps we should continue the family biz. It seems we're meant for the parts."

Abigail frowned. "Henry would turn over in his grave."

"That's an even better reason, dear. It's time he knew you're more than a pretty face." Mildred threw her head back in delighted laughter.

Chapter 28

Another Surprise

Jeremiah patted Mildred on the shoulder. "Millie, Ms. Abigail, this has truly been a remarkable cruise and we're less than a week into a month-long venture. Please try to get a good night's rest. In the morning after breakfast we'll have another little chat. There may even be a reward for the capture of Mr. Modesto. We can discuss the details with the Interpol representative, he'll come aboard in the morning. There's just one thing bothering me. Surely, Modesto didn't act alone on the ship. He seems to have had accomplices in other capers."

Mildred and Abigail shot each other a look, then at the exact same time announced, "Isaac!"

"Who?"

"Remember, when I had forgotten that Ferdinand had our room key and he was passed-out in the infirmary, you called for a master key to our room. The porter who showed up and unlocked our door, that was Isaac. Every time we turn around he's close by. Even Ferdinand said he asked 'a porter' who the *lovely ladies* were. That had to be Isaac."

Jeremiah folded his arms. "Shall we set a snare and see if our bird runs into it?"

Abigail smiled. "Perfect metaphor, dear."

Mildred grinned. "What do you have in mind, Captain Baby?"

He pulled his cell phone from his pocket and dialed. "Yes, Sergeant, would you check Mr. Modesto's cell phone contacts for the name Isaac? — Yes, it's there, okay would you do me the favor of sending a text to that number. — Yes, would you type in, 'The bait is set, join me to spring the trap.'"

Mildred interrupted, "And Ferdinand always taps three times."

"Yes, and add to the text. 'Knock on their door with

my usual greeting and do this immediately, my friend.'
— Yes, send it now, please. Thank you, Sergeant."

Abigail looked bewildered, "What now, Jeremiah?"

"Now we go into your stateroom and wait." He smiled as Mildred scanned the key card.

They barely got the door closed and stepped away when they heard, *tap, tap, tap.*

The Captain stepped forward and turned the knob.

As the door swung open, Isaac's smile turned to horror. "Captain, uh, uh, how can I assist you?"

"You could assist me my marching yourself to the brig."

"But sir, I don't understand."

The Captain placed his hands on his hips. "Why did you come to this door, at this time?"

"I wanted to see if the ladies needed anything?"

"Why did you tap three times?"

"Did I? I, uh …"

"Isaac, hand me your phone."

He turned to run.

"If you run, it will only make the charge stronger against you."

Isaac froze, reached in his pocket and handed his phone to Captain Williams who opened it and read the most recent text.

"Isaac, I'm placing you under arrest until local authorities can come for you. At the very least, you will be charged with aiding in defrauding passengers. You will never work for any ship in the leisure industry again." The Captain turned to the intercom system. "I need two personnel to this location to escort a prisoner to the brig."

Two uniformed officers rushed up.

"Please take, Isaac, I don't know your last name."

"Tompkins, Captain."

"Gentlemen take Mr. Tompkins to the brig and make sure he's guarded until local officials arrive."

Each man took an elbow. "Yes, sir, Captain." They led him away.

Jeremiah returned to the stateroom. "Once again, ladies, your instincts were spot on," he laughed, "anything else you need to tell me?"

Abigail leaned in. "I think you should try to make your food less yummy. I've gained weight. My clothes are getting too tight."

He tossed his head back and laughed.

Mildred chimed in. "I think I've lost weight, my regular clothes are loose, she looked down at her pantsuit, "not these fabulous duds the girls picked, of course, but what I had when we came aboard. I think all this sleuthing is great exercise."

Jeremiah put an arm around each of them. "You girls are amazing. I love you both," and he kissed each on the top of the head.

That reminded Mildred. "You told me if I helped you catch this rascal you'd kiss me on the cheek."

She grinned and tilted her head.

"My pleasure!" and he gave her a big kiss on the cheek.

Her smile lit the room. "Thank you, Jeremiah, I adore you, son."

Chapter 29

Interpol

At breakfast, Jeremiah joined them. "Millie, Ms. Abigail, I'd like you to meet Bryan Saunders. He is acting for the British government as a liaison with Interpol. He has authority to accompany a local Caribbean official to return Ferdinand Modesto to Egypt, the site of his last major crime. There, he will face an International Tribunal and stand trial for crimes committed, including grand theft and taking hostages. From there he will be escorted to London where he will be tried for possession of stolen property, then to Amsterdam, where he will be given a chance to name the original thieves, from whom he stole the Van Gogh, or he will face trial for that theft, as well as several others.

Mr. Saunders I'd like you to meet the ladies of the Fine~Butterfly Detective Agency, Ms. Abigail Fine and Ms. Mildred Butterfly."

He offered his hand to Abigail. "It is a great pleasure to meet such skilled and may I be so bold in this climate of Political Correctness to add, such lovely detectives."

Abigail flashed pink. "Oh, thank you, Mr. Saunders."

"Please call me Bryan." He turned his hand and gaze toward Mildred. "And a pleasure to meet you too, though I hear that congratulations will soon be in order."

"Well, who's passing that rumor?" and she winked at Jeremiah.

The Captain spread his open palm. "Ladies, would you join us in my office?"

The short walk landed them in a nice, but not palatial office, adjacent to the Bridge, Jeremiah closed the door. "Ladies, Mr. Saunders, please take a seat." He pulled a chair from the conference table and held it for Mildred, then one for Abigail.

The agent seated himself across from them.

When the Captain took his seat, he turned to the

liaison. "Saunders, would you like to tell the ladies what you told me earlier?"

"Certainly, it would be my pleasure. Ms. Fine, Ms. Butterfly, due to the information you provided the Captain, we located the stolen Van Gogh in Modesto's flat in London. The museum had offered a substantial reward for its safe return and that reward has never been rescinded. I'm pleased to tell you that you will receive a check from the museum's insurance company in the amount of one million euros."

Abigail clamped her hands to her face. "How much is that in real money?"

The agent and Captain Williams laughed.

Saunders answered, "That would be about one million, one hundred-eighty thousand dollars, at today's exchange rate, but that's not all. The owner of the yacht that was stolen, offered a reward of fifty thousand euros, that would be almost fifty-nine thousand dollars, for the capture of the man who was the mastermind of the theft, whether the yacht was returned or not, I think that was mainly revenge on the thief for deceiving his daughter." He smiled. "In addition, with the other information you supplied, Interpol was able to track several people who were robbed of various artifacts and gold coins. The reward could climb to as much as three million euros and that would be over three million, five hundred thousand," he chuckled, "in real money."

Mildred's mouth dropped open. "You mean we're millionaires?"

Abigail patted her face with her fingertips. "Millie, am I dreaming?"

Jeremiah reached for one of her hands, held it in his and smiled. "No, Ms. Abby, you aren't dreaming. You both have done a world-class job and you deserve the reward." He took Millie's hand with his other. "You two are brilliant and I'm so proud of you. Millie, you spotted him as a fake from the beginning and together you have also spared our cruise-line from being sued by others who have been fleeced by Modesto and I have another surprise for you after lunch. May I suggest you go have your hair done and perhaps buy a new frock?" and he laughed.

Mildred's chair pushed back from the table. "Agent Saunders, Jeremiah, I don't know what to say. I started out merely trying to protect my sister—who knew how this would turn out?"

Chapter 30

Straight to the Salon

Appointments were scheduled, Shell and Becca stood ready. "Good morning ladies."

Shell continued. "We have been given instructions by the Captain, please be seated."

Abigail lifted her hands. "What on earth is going on?"

Becca took her hand and spun her toward the chair. "All we can tell you is that there will be a surprise after lunch and you are to be gussied-up, but not too fru-fru."

Mildred frowned. "What on earth does that mean?"

Shell laughed. "Now don't you be concerned, haven't we always treated you right?"

Abigail sighed. "Oh, Millie, relax. We always love

what these girls do for us."

"Okay, but I'm not too sure about 'gussied' and 'fru-fru,' what do those terms even mean?"

An hour later, the chairs turned.

"Abigail, we look just like we did after our first appointment. My curls cascade in loops in the back from the crown of my head, down to my collar. The top and sides are smooth and soft, at angles toward the front and sides of my face. My makeup brightens my face and the colors highlight my eyes and lips."

Just as before, Abigail's short, perky hair framed her face with a pixie-like effect. It was still gray, but came to a point on each cheek, next to the bottom of her ears.

"And Abby, your eyes gleam, the effect is dramatic, but still somehow subtle."

Shell asked, "Would you say you are gussied, but not too fru-frued?"

She and Becca laughed.

Becca continued, now to the dress shop ladies.

Abigail sighed, "Do we really need new frocks?"

The girls removed the salon capes and Shell lifted her

hand toward the door. "We have our orders, ladies."

Mildred folded her arms across her middle and bristled. "Who exactly is giving these orders?"

Shell replied, "You don't want to get us fired, now do you?"

Mildred's arms dropped to her sides. "Of course not, sweetie, you have both been nothing but fabulous to us." She breathed out a big gust. "Okay, lead the way. We're in your hands."

At the dress shop, outfits were pulled and handed to them.

The first one out of the dressing room, as usual, was Abigail. A short-sleeved white silk blouse topped lime green capris. "Hurry up Millie, what's taking you so long? I need your opinion."

"They've given me one of those rubber tube-thingies again. You know that takes a minute to wriggle into." Finally, Mildred pushed the door open. "Okay, let me see how you look, Abby."

As she approached, Abigail raised her eyes to look over her shoulder at Mildred's reflection.

"Millie, you look amazing." She whirled toward her sister. "Are your trousers silk? They're exquisite and that blouse! That outfit looks like it was made for you."

Cream-colored, trim-fitting, silk trousers, topped by a vibrant pink, silk shirt tapered at the waist, reflected the light coming in through the window.

Abigail yielded way to her sister.

Stepping before the mirror, Mildred's eyes teared. "I can't believe this, I'm wearing light colored pants and they're a size smaller than I normally wear. What's going on here?"

Her sister came up beside her. "I think you've lost the doldrums and you're feeling more like your former self."

"Abby, I never knew how depressed I was. When I lost Max, I thought my life was over, but I was so busy trying to watch-out for you, I let myself go, terribly."

"We both did, dear. Our husbands had been the joy of our lives for forty-five years. We were so impacted by the loss, we couldn't crawl out from under it. In spite of the fact that we caught a criminal, we both needed this trip. Having these two geniuses," she peered into the mirror at Shell and Becca, "put us together helped us realize we can still feel pretty and enjoy our lives."

Mildred turned. "You girls had better run or you're going to get hugged."

Shell and Becca stepped toward Mildred and Abigail.

Shell stuck out her arms. "We're not going to run, give us a hug. You're the most amazing ladies we've met, since our mom."

Hugs all around, spilled over to the lady who ran the dress shop. She didn't seem to mind.

Becca stepped back and passed out tissues. "Ms. Mildred and Ms. Abigail, you are so much fun and so loving, it has been our pleasure. Now, would you like for us to drop off the clothes you wore in today or are you heading back to your room?"

"We'll take them, dear." Mildred reached for the clothes that had been carefully folded and bagged. "I have a pair of earrings I'd like to get from our room."

"Special, are they?" Shell smiled.

"They're simple little things, teardrop-shaped with one pink opal, surrounded by cubic zirconia stones, but I was wearing them the day Maxwell proposed to me. I've held onto them all these years, but I didn't think I'd ever wear them again after Max died. For some reason, I think today calls for a fresh start."

Abigail nodded. "I think that's a grand idea, Millie and they would look perfect with that outfit."

The dress store clerk, usually quiet, began to weep. "That is so sweet. You'd better run now, you don't want to be late."

Shell patted the clerk on the back, then turned. "Yes, ladies, you need to scurry, I'll take care of Victoria."

Chapter 31

Tell Us!

At lunch, Jeremiah joined them. "Ladies, once again you look astounding. I hope you're enjoying your meal."

Mildred lifted her face and smiled at him. "We are, dear."

Abigail interrupted. "But tell us what the surprise is!"

He tilted his head and laughed. "When you're finished eating, we'll walk out on the fantail and you'll experience the surprise."

They looked at each other. "Experience? The surprise."

Jeremiah sat down. "Yes, be patient a little bit longer and finish your meal."

A folded napkin hit Abigail's plate. "Hurry up, Millie, I want to know what's going on."

Mildred chuckled. "Well, Jeremiah, I think I'm finished or there won't be any peace around here."

He stood and placed his hand on the back of Mildred's chair to assist her. "Very well ladies," he looked through the back window. "I think everything is ready. This way, please." He reached for the door, held it open and tipped his hat onto his head.

Abigail rushed through and passed her sister, Jeremiah came up beside Mildred, placed his hand on her back and led them to a shaded area. "Ladies, allow me to introduce my daughters, Shelly and Rebecca." Jeremiah lifted his hand and motioned for them to come over.

The two stylists from the salon walked up.

Abigail blinked. "You girls are our hair dressers."

Jeremiah smiled. "And your guardian angels. They've been shadowing you to watch over you."

Mildred smiled. "These girls are marvels with hair and makeup."

He waved again. "And allow me to introduce my father." A very handsome man approached. "This is my dad, George Williams."

When he was closer Mildred recognized him. "Aren't you the man I saw across the room at the dance and down the street from the Beach Comber?" She cut her eyes to Jeremiah. "Why didn't you introduce us earlier?"

The man lifted his hand and a smooth, pleasant voice mesmerized them. "Good afternoon, ladies. It's a pleasure to meet you again."

Mildred tipped her head. "Again, have we met before?"

He reached in his mouth and removed a partial plate, stooped his shoulders a little and laughed a familiar shrill *he he he*. "Yes, girlie, we've met before."

Mildred's and Abigail's eyes popped open wide and their lower jaws dropped.

Mildred shouted, "Cranky Pants, is that you?"

He replaced his partial and pushed his shoulders back. "Yes, Millie, it's me."

"But I don't understand, Cranky."

His smooth voice returned. "The night you called me, I was surprised because I had forgotten that the listing for Cranky Pants Plumbing was in the phonebook, my wife had placed it in there as a joke long before she died. You see, I had been a plumber for years, but I continually invested in something she wasn't sure was a good idea. She tried to get me to stop, but I refused, so she dubbed me Cranky Pants. When I saw the name, Fine~Butterfly Detective Agency, on my Caller I.D., I thought God was answering a prayer for me. You see, I'm part owner of this cruise line and we'd had reports of passengers, ladies, being taken advantage of by a conman. I hadn't thought of hiring a private detective, but when I heard your voice, I made a quick decision. Then when I met you two lovely ladies, I knew you were the private detectives we needed."

Mildred paused, then laughed. "But Cranky Pants," she looked at her sister, "we aren't detectives, that was our husbands, Maxwell and Henry. We just haven't had the heart to take the sign down."

Jeremiah, George and the girls laughed.

George pushed his shoulders up. "Whether you knew it or not, you *are* detectives and you girls are good. I've watched your progress and you're amazing. At the beach, that little romp in the water was, well, let's just call it inspiring."

Abigail yelled, "No! Tell me you didn't see that? I'm horrified."

Mildred patted her arm and laughed. "Hush dear, he was inspired. Let the gentleman talk." Another thought hit her. "Oh, my goodness, was that sales girl at the Beach Comber one of your granddaughters too?"

George's family laughed, but he answered. "No, that was a stroke of luck. Wait, let me rephrase that, I think that was the Lord too. She was really good and that sarong, Millie, ooo-la-la." He smiled.

Mildred's face flashed hot. "Stop it, George."

He grinned. "That's the first time you've used my real name."

"Well, if you want me to keep using your *real name*, you'll hire that girl and put in a swimwear shop on the ship."

"Consider it done, my dear."

Mildred's eyebrows pushed together. "Your, dear?"

"Yes, my dear, I would like to court you for the rest of the cruise and if you decide I'm worthy, I would like to marry you. Jeremiah can perform the ceremony before we arrive home, while we're still in International Waters."

Mildred shouted, "Marry you?" She glanced over at Jeremiah.

"Don't look at me, Millie, the girls and I have voted and you're already a member of the family."

Shell and Becca smiled and shook their head.

She shouted again, "Marry you!"

He reached in his pocket and produced a small box, opened it and a one carat diamond glistened in the sunlight. "Yes, dear, but if you decide against marrying me, they can bury me at sea, because I shall die of a broken heart. I've fallen madly in love with you, Mildred Butterfly, you are the most lovely and amazing woman I've met since I lost my precious wife, Shelly." He lifted her left hand and slid the ring on.

Abigail giggled. "I can hear the wedding vows now; do you, Cranky Pants take Grumpy Britches to be your lawfully wedded wife?"

Everyone else laughed while Mildred stammered. "But, but …"

"But what, my dear?"

She glanced at her sister. "But I can't leave Abby."

Abigail's eyes flew open wide. "Are you kidding? Don't try to use me as an excuse."

George cradled her hand in his. "We can solve that problem too, Millie. Abigail can live with us, or we can find her a husband, I happen to know of a doctor who's taken quite an interest in your *fine* sister."

Abigail joined her sister in stammering. "Who? What?"

George turned his gaze to Abigail. "And I can assure you Dr. Fielding is a fine man, Ms. Abby. I've known him for years, he's my brother-in-law, my late wife's brother."

Chapter 32

Our Dates

That evening the cabin door announced their visitors. *Knock, knock, knock.*

Wearing a lovely turquoise dress, Mildred stepped forward and opened the door. "Hello, George, good evening, Dr. Fielding."

"Please, Ms. Butterfly, call me Sam."

"Only if you call me Mildred."

Dr. Fielding nodded. "Deal."

Mildred smiled and looked over her shoulder. "Abigail, our dates are here,"iv she chuckled. "My, how strange that sounds."

A muffled reply from the bathroom, "I'll only be a moment."

"Gentlemen, would you like to come in, we could wait on the terrace?"

George laughed. "I've never actually sat on one of the patios before, that might be nice." They stepped inside and George led the way to the sliding glass door. He opened it and the cool evening breeze met his face. "This would seem to be a nice night for a walk on deck after dinner. Would that be okay with you, Millie?"

"It sounds wonderful, but first I have to make it through the meal at the Captain's Table without spilling something on myself, I'm actually quite nervous."

George laughed. "Relax, Millie, you're not on trial here, I am. I've seen you at your worst," he arched one eyebrow, "under the spray of the kitchen faucet and at your best," he wiggled both eyebrows, "playing the part of a femme fatale, the man eater, on the beach with Ferdinand."

A nervous laugh erupted from Mildred. "Yes, but the first was an accident and the second was an act. I don't really know who I am in a new relationship. I haven't dated since I was a teen and even then, I didn't date much."

"That makes us even." George tried to encourage her. "The first time we met, I was playing a part, remember Mr. Cranky Pants? The second time was sort of an accident, because I thought you and Abigail were detectives. Thinking back, I have to laugh at myself, I thought that God was answering my prayer about finding the gigolo on the ship." He laughed and it lit her soul.

Sam joined the laughter. "Perhaps God *was* answering your prayer, George and he answered one you just hadn't thought to pray yet. You were so devoted to my sister that you couldn't imagine having a life with anyone else."

The bathroom door opened, their heads turned.

Abigail stepped out in a bright, red dress. "I think I'm as together as I can get, doing it myself." Her hair was neatly styled, but not lavish, her makeup was lightly applied, actually barely visible.

Sam stood. "Ms. Abigail, you look marvelous."

She smiled and tipped her head toward one shoulder. "Thank you, doctor, but if we are going to start off right, please, call me Abby."

He nodded in agreement. "Then you call me Sam."

George lifted his hand in the familiar palm-up, crew-style directive. "Ladies, Sam, shall we make our way to the dining room?" He closed the patio door.

Sam walked to the front door, opened it and held his arm up for Abigail.

"Thank you, Sam, how sweet."

Mildred stepped into the corridor behind them, followed by George who closed the door.

"Millie, could I convince you to take my arm as well?"

She smiled and reached for his elbow.

"Millie, you're trembling."

"I know George, I'm sorry, I feel like I have to be something I'm not."

"What is it, my dear? Have I put too much pressure on you? I know that you are the most unique woman I've ever met. You're charming, funny and heaven knows I'm no match for you in the brains department."

"Stop it George! I think you're marvelous. To be honest, I started falling in love with you as Cranky Pants. Now that I know you're so sophisticated and handsome, I'm a little undone."

He stepped to the side and paused. "Millie! You said you starting falling in love with me as Cranky Pants, do I have to live without my partial plate in my mouth and stoop my shoulders to keep your heart? I will, if I need to."

She swatted his arm. "No, of course not."

They continued to walk.

"It was the romantic notion of you working behind the scenes fiddling things into place. It was a romantic notion that I never dreamed I'd be confronted with."

"So, you fell in love with Cyrano de Bergerac, but this time the fellow you loved turned out to be both the ugly Cyrano and the Baron. My, what a predicament." He laughed. "Whom will you choose?" He smiled and glanced at her face, but saw tears. "Millie, what is it? Did my silly rambling offend you?" He handed her his pocket handkerchief.

"No, George, it quite aptly put into words what I hadn't yet realized. I fell for your Cyrano, Mr. Cranky Pants, because of his personality and his care of all the details behind our intrigue, but now that I know you're the Baron, I don't feel worthy of loving you. I feel so inadequate, so unlovable."

"Millie, don't be ridiculous, dear, I saw you for who you are. I fell in love with the real you."

"But was that the real me, George, or was it an actor on a stage?"

George stopped and stepped in front of Mildred. "Millie, when I told you my name was George and you persisted in calling me Cranky Pants. I loved it. When my son told you to call him Jeremiah or he would have to insist you called him Captain Baby—well, we know how that turned out—I fell more deeply in love. Your sense of humor is so winning for me. Without knowing it I'd allowed myself to wallow in depression and self-pity, you began to chip away at that. When I saw your theatrics with Ferdinand, I was bursting inside with laughter, partially because it was funny that you were making the man squirm, but partly because it was genius. The plans you laid and even when you had to improvise threw a spotlight on your brilliance. Millie, that's what I love about you and that can't be faked."

Mildred dissolved into tears, spread his handkerchief on the shoulder of his white jacket and sobbed into it.

He embraced her and patted her back.

When she lifted her head, he was smiling.

"See what I mean, darling, the very act of covering my clothes to keep from getting makeup on me, you're adorable, you're funny, you're touching and I love you."

She cried and buried her face again in the handkerchief covered shoulder.

When she recovered, she wiped her eyes and said, "George, I need to go back to the room and fix my face."

"If you wish dear, I'll go ahead and tell Sam and Abby that you'll only be a minute." He strode off toward the dining hall.

Mildred turned toward the room. When she reached the door, she was searching in her purse for the key when a black bag flew over her head. She struggled, but two men held her tight. "Isaac, is that you?"

A gruff voice replied, "Do you think Isaac was the only one?"

Chapter 33

Two Brutes

Mildred struggled against the two men, but her strength was not equal to theirs. She knew the layout of the ship well enough by now to realize she had been hustled into an unfamiliar passageway. At a flight of stairs, they pushed her hands onto a metal handrail, one man went before her, another after. She used her feet to feel for the next rung, then the next. Not quite vertical, but far steeper than regular stairs, she descended into blackness, engine noises whined, becoming more prevalent. Her mind raced for a plan. At the bottom of the stairs she steadied herself. "What do you want with me?"

The deeper voice growled. "Shut up, big mouth. We,

don't want you."

"Then why have you hijacked me? Where are we going?"

A younger voice sputtered. "The boss wants to see you."

Mildred stiffened. "The boss, you mean Ferdinand?"

The younger voice laughed. "Ferdinand, you've gotta be kiddin' me. He was a nobody, a loser, he answered to the boss."

"Who's the boss."

The gruff voice laughed, then growled again. "Do you really expect us to tell you a name, lady. Are you stoopid or somethin'?"

Mildred fought against panic. "Well, where's the boss? And what does he want with me."

One of the men grabbed her hands and began to zip-tie them in front of her, then tied them to the rail. Footsteps trailed away from her.

"Hello, hello, are you still here?"

No answer came.

She lifted her voice. "Help! Hello!" but no response. The noise of the engine drowned-out her voice.

Think Millie, think. If no one can hear you, you need to save your voice. I can hardly breathe with this heavy hood on.

She leaned toward her bound hands, grabbed the top of the bag at the front of her head and eased it up. She gasped for air when it cleared her nose and mouth. *A little bit further.* Her eyes squinted when the light hit them. Machinery and heavy metal pipes surrounded her except for a narrow walkway along the wall behind her. The black hood rested on the top of her head, just above her ears. *If I pull this thing off and they come back, they'll probably kill me because I saw their faces. What to do? Father, what do I do?*

Mildred pulled the hood off with her tied hands, then bent to grab it with her teeth. *If I can tear some small holes in this then get it back on my head, that might help.* She positioned the hood where she thought her eyes might be when she donned it again and with an eyetooth began to gnaw at the thick fabric. Finally, one hole! She turned the mask slightly and again with the eyetooth gnawed a small hole.

The sound of footsteps prodded her. *I've got to get*

this back on. She pulled it from her mouth and held it with her fingertips, *Help me, Father!* She wiggled her head and the cloth began to slip over her hair, then over her eyes and down her nose. Just as it reached her chin, the two thugs returned.

"Hey, what you doin'?" asked the gruff voice.

"I'm having trouble breathing! I'm trying to get more air."

The younger man with slim hands reached for the bottom of the hood and pulled it away from her face. "Is that better?"

"Yes, thank you!"

One eyehole was in position, but the other was askew. Still, she could see a little. "What are you going to do with me? You know I'm supposed to be at the Captain's Table tonight. I'll be missed soon and they'll start looking."

The gruff voiced man grumbled, "I said, shut up, broad!" but she wasn't expecting the punch she received in her side. A groan escaped as her knees buckled beneath her. Half kneeling, half dangling by her lashed wrists, she gulped for air. "Now, stay there, the boss is on his way."

The door at the top of the stairs opened and closed quickly.

Mildred fought for breath following the blow, she tipped her head to try to center the hood's tiny hole over her eye and leaned her head back.

White uniform trousers came into view. "What did you do to her, Moose? She's got to be in good enough shape to move her, unless you want to carry her."

"No, boss, sorry."

The man's voice was familiar. She'd heard it before, but where? Who?

"One of you go get the car and bring it alongside the luggage bay."

"Yes, sir, boss!" The younger man's footsteps bounded down the narrow aisle along the bulkhead.

"Get her to the cargo door, Moose and no more messing around."

The man cut her zip-tie that held her to the rail and pulled her elbow. "Get up, big mouth and no more chatter out of you."

She moaned as he pulled her to her feet.

Her side throbbed, but her breathing had almost returned to normal.

Chapter 34

The Alarm

George dashed into the dining room and raced to his son's table, leaned to his ear and whispered, "Jeremiah, help me! Millie's missing. Her purse and its contents were strewn on the floor in front of her suite, the room is empty, but there was a ransom note on the door!"

Jeremiah bolted upright, scooting his chair back. "Ladies and gentlemen, please excuse us. Doctor, Ms. Abby, we need you, now!"

Sam grabbed the back of Abigail's chair and pulled her away from the table.

She jumped up. "But what's wrong?"

"Come on, Abby, I've known George and Jeremiah

long enough to know not to ask." He took Abigail by the arm and pursued after them, hauling her along.

Outside the door, the Captain picked up an intercom handset. "To all hands, this is the Captain. Seal all exits! Security, this is a possible Live Fire Scenario, man your stations. This is not a drill, I repeat, this is not a drill." He turned to his dad, as Sam and Abigail arrived. "We have to cover the exits immediately. Dad, come with me. Doctor, take Ms. Abby back to her room and stay with her, Millie has gone missing."

Abigail threw her hands to her mouth and squealed.

Jeremiah and George raced to the main entrance. The watchman jerked to attention. "What is it, Captain? I heard the alert."

Security arrived.

"A passenger is missing, presumed to have been taken forcibly. Has anyone left this way in the last twenty minutes?"

"Only a few passengers, sir, but no one who looked under duress."

"Do you know Ms. Mildred Butterfly?"

"Yes, sir, I've met her."

"Has she been through here?"

"No, sir, absolutely not."

"Stay right here. No one, I repeat, no one, leaves without my clearance."

"Yes, sir."

Jeremiah looked at his dad. "We need to access the security cameras. Follow me." They raced to the Communications Room, he threw the door open. "Show me all CCTV footage for the last twenty-five minutes, start with the hallway outside the Princess Suite first."

"Yes, sir." He worked the controls.

Video scrolled.

"Stop there!"

The film showed two masked men forcing a hood over Mildred's head.

George gasped and threw his hand over his mouth.

Jeremiah placed his hand on his father's shoulder. "Steady, Dad. Crewman, scroll forward. Where did they take her?"

Video revealed the passageway and the crew hatch. "Any cameras through there?"

"Already on it, Captain." The crewman pulled up a

different camera, the footage showed Mildred forced down the steps, strapped to the rail, then the unexpected blow to her side.

Tears welled up in George's eyes.

The Captain, still very much in command, "Scroll forward, which way did they go?"

The camera revealed they exited down the narrow passage.

"No cameras there, Captain," the crewman looked at a schematic, "but only three possible exits."

"Show me!"

Route one revealed no people present during the time frame. The second route revealed several crewmen at work. "No way they went through there, sir. Only one more possibility." He worked the controls. "The luggage bay, sir."

The video raced forward, showing the two men forcing Mildred down the luggage ramp. "Sir that should never have been open while we were docked. This had to be planned."

Captain Williams leaned over the man's shoulder. "Show me the coverage of the dock."

The screen switched and was rewound to the approximate time. "Captain, it's a taxi, but the number's been covered. They shoved her in the trunk, sir."

The timestamp revealed the exact time.

He turned to George. "Dad, my security order was two minutes too late, but we have information." He turned to the crewman. "Get me the local police on the phone."

The crewman picked up the com-phone, scrambled to dial the local authorities and handed the receiver to him.

Two rings, then, "Yes, this is Captain Williams of the cruise ship Princess of the Sea. I need your help, we've had a kidnapping. — Yes, about thirty minutes ago. — Yes, you've met the victim, Ms. Mildred Butterfly. I fear this may be connected to the arrest of Modesto. — Yes, she was taken by two masked men and bundled into a taxi, but the number was covered and Sergeant, they're not afraid to use force. We know that she was punched in the ribs once, it was caught on CCTV. The taxi left the Princess at six-eighteen local time. — Yes, my father and I will join you on this one. Could you send a car for us as soon as possible, but please scan your footage to see if you can tell where they've gone. This one is personal, Sergeant." Jeremiah handed the receiver to the crewman. "Please cancel the alert and have security stand down. Notify the Chief Mate that my father and I are going ashore."

"Yes, sir, Captain."

They reached the gangway as a Police car slid to a stop on the dock.

The Captain and George raced down the steps, a local officer opened the door for them and they jumped in.

"We'll be at the station in two minutes sir."

Lights flashed and the siren blared.

Jeremiah put his hand on his dad's shoulder. "Dad, are you okay?"

"I'm not sure, Jeremiah, I should never have left her alone."

"Dad, you can't go there. You know as well as I do, cruise ships are the safest vacation a person can take. This is linked to Modesto. It has to be."

"I know, son," he looked into Jeremiah's eyes, "but

I'm the one who sicked-her-on-him. It's my fault and I just can't lose her."

"It's not your fault and you won't lose her, Dad. Not if I have anything to do with it. Now, calm yourself and let Ms. Abby know what's happening."

George pulled out his cellphone and dialed.

Abigail's phone barely rang. "Hello, George," her voice was frantic, "what's happening?"

"We're tracking Mildred."

She screamed. "Tracking her where?"

"Give the phone to Sam, please, Abby. — Yes, Sam, this is the situation."

As he explained, the police car jerked to a stop in the parking lot.

"I'll keep you informed, Sam, but don't leave Abigail's side. You might want to give her a sedative, you be the judge. I've gotta run."

Inside the Station

The Sergeant motioned for them to join him in a glass-encased room.

"Captain, Mr. Williams, we picked them up as they left the dock and followed them through town. When they took the Coast Road we lost them."

"Where does that road go?" asked George.

"There are many homes of locals out that way and further on it goes into a forest that's allocated for conservation."

The Sergeant turned to a map on the wall. "This is where we are," then he traced a road along the shoreline. "This was the route they took, and this," he tapped, "is the area that is under conservation control, but here," and he circled an area, "this is the most likely place if they're holding her in a house." He turned to face Jeremiah, "Captain, have you thought of the possibility of her being taken by boat to a different island?"

George turned away, faced the floor and ran his hands through his hair.

The Sergeant noticed and asked, "Captain, you said, this is personal."

He nodded. "My dad had hoped to marry Mildred on this cruise."

George jerked around, "Not *hoped* to marry her, no,

I'm going to marry her. We have to find her. We need to get out there."

"Mr. Williams, my men are already in the area. They know the people and can be discreet. If anyone knows anything, they'll find out." He turned to Jeremiah, "Captain, may I make a suggestion?"

"Certainly!"

"However, you could accomplish this, try to quietly find out if you have any crewmen missing. I'm certain this didn't start from the outside. Getting aboard would have been too dangerous. Getting her off would have been more easily accomplished by crewmen familiar with the ship."

"That's very logical, Sergeant. I'm afraid, I'm out of my depth in this."

Jeremiah reached for his cellphone and dialed.

The phone rang and a crewman in the communications room answered.

"This is the Captain, connect me with the Chief Mate, he should be on the Bridge. — Chief, I'm ashore assisting the local police in searching for Ms. Butterfly, she was kidnapped earlier this evening. — Yes, shocking. Now I need you to quietly start contacting department heads and get them to do a check of all personnel. Let me know who's absent without cause and notify me immediately if you get a ransom call. — Thank you. I'll check back in a couple of hours." He lowered the receiver to its cradle.

"Sergeant, what can we do to help?"

"Does the lady's family know of the situation?"

"Yes, but we probably do need to give an update." He turned to George, "Dad, are you up to this, or should I?"

George pulled his cellphone and pressed redial. It rang a half a ring and Sam answered.

"Sam, how's Abby? — Good, she needs the rest. We're here with the local authorities, they tracked the taxi that was used and they're already canvassing the area in question. Keep Abby safe for us. — Thanks, Sam. — Yeah, we'll keep in touch." He closed his phone. "Sergeant, have you contacted the cab company to see if a car is missing?"

"Yes, sir, Mr. Williams. Many drivers take their cabs home when they're off duty."

Jeremiah rubbed his chin. "Can we get a list of the off-duty cabbies and do a little sleuthing?"

The Sergeant pulled up an email and hit print. The printer whirred and spit out a fresh sheet. "Would you like to join me, gentlemen?"

Jeremiah pulled his hat from under his arm. "Lead the way, please."

At the squad car, the Sergeant held the door for Jeremiah and George, then got behind the wheel. "Gentlemen, should we start at the farthest point and work back toward town? Or work our way out."

George leaned forward, "It would seem logical to take her as far away from the ship as possible. Doesn't it?"

"Yes, but that's only if the house that's the furthest away belonged to one of the culprits."

"Is there a way to check the homes' ownership against my ship's roster?"

He nodded. "Certainly, if you can get us the list."

Jeremiah pulled his cellphone and dialed. "This is the Captain, I need a full roster, officers and crew, emailed to the local police department. — Yes, immediately." He replaced his phone in his inside pocket.

The Sergeant cranked the car and switched on his radio. "This is car one. We're heading west, but expect an email from the Princess and check their crew roster against local land deeds. Let me know as soon as you find anything."

The car zipped through town and along the coast road.

"Our first cabbie lives just ahead." The Sergeant slowed the car and turned into a sandy driveway.

The taxi driver was washing his cab, but looked up.

George grabbed the back of the front seat. "Could he be trying to destroy evidence?"

"Take it easy, Mr. Williams, let me check it out." He stepped from behind the wheel. "Good evening, sir, are you Mr. Ramos?"

"Yes, how can I help you?"

"Sir, we're looking for a missing lady. She was taken from the docks by a taxi. Can you help us with that?"

"I would gladly, if I could, but I had a group of

tourists in my cab and one of them got sick so I had to deliver them to their destination and log out for the day. I've been cleaning ever since."

The Sergeant turned his cap in his hand. "Can you tell me where you dropped them and what time?"

"Sure, let me grab my log sheet. — Hard to forget them, I dropped them at the Ambassador Hotel, there were three of them, let me see, yes, it was at half past five. I'm sure the doorman will remember, they reeked of vomit. Not easy to forget." He smiled.

"Thank you, Mr. Ramos and before we go, have you seen anything suspicious?"

"A taxi did whip past here, not long after I got home."

"Can you tell us anything about the cab or the driver?"

"No, sorry, I had my back turned, I only saw a glimpse, just enough to know it was one of my company's cars. I wondered what the hurry was."

The Sergeant turned toward the squad car, then Ramos caught his attention.

"Excuse me, a picture of the taxi just flashed into my

mind, the back, passenger light cover was broken."

"Thank you! Here's my card, please call the office if you hear or remember anything else. Thanks again."

He jumped into the car and turned to look in the backseat. "Was she placed in the trunk?"

George flung himself toward the front seat. "Yes, she was, does he know where she is"

"No, but we're on the right track, a cab with a broken light cover flew past here about the right time to fit the timetable."

George slapped the back of the seat. "That's my girl, she broke their taillight. She's smart."

The officer nodded. "Indeed, but we need to be methodical in our search." He picked up the radio. "This is car one. Tell the men to look for a taxi with a broken, passenger-side taillight." He looked in his rearview mirror. "Gentlemen do you need any coffee?"

George shook his head. "No, we need to keep going."

"Mr. Williams, it's going to be dark soon and I could use some coffee to keep me sharp. Can't I get you something?"

Jeremiah nodded. "You're right of course, Dad also

missed dinner."

He snapped. "I can't eat anything while Millie is out there!"

"Well, Dad, let's allow the Sergeant to get some coffee."

"There's a roadside stand right down the way. The owner is my brother-in-law, he might have seen the cab." He started the engine.

Seconds later they pulled over at a cabana. "I'll only be a moment."

"Dad do you need to stretch your legs, this could be a long night."

"If Millie is cramped into the trunk of a taxi, I'm sure I'll be fine back here."

Jeremiah patted his dad's arm. "We don't know that she's still in the trunk. Think positive."

"I'm positive of one thing, I'm never going to let her out of my sight again, whether she marries me or not."

Jeremiah smiled. "That could be a little difficult, Dad. You know how independent Millie is."

The Sergeant returned with three cups of coffee.

"Just in case, gentlemen and there's cream and sugar in the bag."

George leaned forward. "Did he know anything?"

"Yes, as a matter of fact, he said he'd seen a stray taxi around these parts a few times in the past week."

Jeremiah reached for a coffee. "That coincides with the arrival of the Princess of the Sea. Did he have any idea where the taxi is hanging-out?"

"Many of the locals come here in the mornings for breakfast and coffee on their way into town. There was some gossip about strangers meeting at a house down on the Cove Road. It's dark enough now that we could go down, but we'd have to walk. Our headlights would be spotted a mile away. Let me radio in to give them our location." He took a sip of coffee and reached for the handheld mic. "This is car one. We're at Brody's Shack, word is there are strangers on the Cove Road. We're heading there now. Any officers in the area can join us, but no lights."

"Roger, Sarge."

"Now, let's get a little sip of coffee for energy, but let's allow some of our emotional juices to calm a bit, okay, Mr. Williams. Too much emotion could put Ms. Butterfly and us in more danger. Cool heads, okay?"

George took a drink of coffee and nodded. "Just tell us what you want us to do."

"We'll ease down this road to the cut-off, then park the car and walk, it's maybe a mile down to the bay. We won't be able to use flashlights either, so you'll have to allow your eyes to adjust to the darkness. We don't want to go charging down there. Got it?"

Jeremiah nodded and placed his hand on his dad's back. "We've got it. Right, Dad?"

George slumped back against the seat "Got it."

"Dad, I'll call the ship and give my officer an update, maybe you should give Sam a call and check on Abby before we go."

Jeremiah pulled out his phone, "This is the Captain, give me the Bridge. — Chief we have a lead. We're going to head to Cove Road. Any news of missing crewmen? — Okay, I'll keep you posted."

George reached in his pocket and pulled out his phone again. He hit redial and heard Sam's voice. "Hi Sam. — No, but we have a lead. We're on the Coast

Road. Someone spotted strangers near here, so we're going to check it out. — Yes, Jeremiah and I are still with the Sergeant. How's Abby? — Okay, good, take care of her."

"What did he say, Dad?"

"Abigail is still sleeping, he has her in the infirmary. He has a nurse with him to help if he needs it. She'll probably be waking up shortly and he'll decide then whether to sedate her for the night or not."

"Good. Uncle Sam's a good man."

George chuckled. "He always hated it when you called him that. Said it made him think of the old guy on the posters, with the long white beard and wearing the red, white and blue outfit."

Jeremiah grinned. "Well, he is my uncle and his name *is* Sam. That's not my fault."

The engine started again and they rolled down the Coast Road. A couple of miles later they came to the cut-off.

The Sergeant turned off the headlights, then he reached over the mirror and turned off the inside light, so it wouldn't come on when the doors were opened.

"Okay, Captain, Mr. Williams, we're going to ease out of the car, no fast moves, no slamming doors, then we're going to stand still for a few minutes. This has to be smooth or we'll tip our hand."

Chapter 35

In the Infirmary

Back on the ship, in the infirmary, Sam sat in a chair next to the bed, holding Abigail's hand.

She began to stir. "Where am I?"

The doctor leaned in close, "You're in the infirmary, Abby."

"Why am I …," she tried to sit up.

"Do you remember tonight at dinner?" He patted her hand gently.

"George came dashing in and Jeremiah …." She pushed herself up. "Millie, where's Millie?"

"Shhh, shhh, lie back and don't get excited."

"But Millie, have they found her?"

"Not yet, my dear, but George, Jeremiah and the

local police are looking for her." He turned to the nurse. "Please, bring Ms. Fine a glass of cold water with a straw."

"Yes, sir, Dr. Fielding." She scurried away.

Abigail tried to push up again, but was too weak. "What's wrong with me?"

"I had to give you a sedative. It was mild, but hasn't worn off completely yet. Just try to relax."

She stared into his eyes. "I can't relax, I have to find my sister."

The nurse returned and handed the water to Dr. Fielding.

He pushed it toward Abigail and held the straw. "Take a sip of water, that sedative has made your throat dry."

She sipped as directed.

When she finished, Sam pulled the glass away and placed it on the cabinet next to the bed. He pushed the remote to raise the head of the bed. "Now are you going to be able to stay calm or will I have to sedate you for the rest of the night?" He tenderly lifted her hand again.

"I'll try, Sam, but I'm so worried. What time is it?"

"It's just after ten."

"I've been out for nearly four hours and Millie's been out there all alone." She began to weep.

"Nurse, prepare a syringe, a full dose this time."

Abigail shook her head. "No, Sam, please wait. I want to be conscious. I'll try not to panic, but," her eyes met his, "she's my sister and my best friend, now she's out there and I can't do anything to help her." She leaned into Sam's shoulder and cried.

"That's fine Abby, but if I see that it's getting to be too much for you, I'll insist on the medication. Okay?"

She pushed away from his shoulder, wiped her eyes with her free hand and leaned back on the bed. "Yes, Sam, okay, but can you tell me what you know?"

For the next half hour, Sam went through the details that he knew. The whole time he held Abigail's hand.

Chapter 36

Cove Road

The Sergeant, Jeremiah and George stood next to the patrol car. Their eyes began to pick out details they'd missed in the beginning.

The Sergeant motioned and they started moving.

Jeremiah whispered, "I hadn't realized we are on a hill."

The Sergeant replied, "Yes, the gradual climb is barely noticeable, but we are on the volcano end of the island." They snuck slowly down the grade, just as it began to sprinkle. "Careful, this will become very slippery."

The rain suddenly increased to a deluge.

JUNE WHATLEY

Inside the Cabin

The roof above Mildred's head began to leak. Water trickled down the hood that still hung over her face. She reached with her fingertips to slide the bag up, tilted her head back and opened her mouth to catch the dribble. She swallowed. "Thank you, Father, you're my source, my protection and my supply. Be with George, Father. If he loves me as much as he says, I know he and Jeremiah are trying to find me and George is probably worried. I know I would be if it were him missing." She chuckled softly. "I guess it took this for me to realized that I do love him."

A phone rang in the other room. Moose's gruff voice answered. "Yes, boss, where to? — Right. Got it." The phone clicked off. "Hey kid, grab the broad."

"What's up?"

"They're on to us, we gotta move."

The door to the room where she was held, flung open. The smaller hands grabbed her by the arm. "Why's your hood up?" Rain dripped on his hand.

"I was thirsty and God supplied me with water."

"Nonsense, lady. Now get up, we gotta move." He jerked the hood down over her mouth.

Mildred twisted her head in the direction of his voice. "You won't win, you know?"

He laughed. "What makes you think that?"

"Because I've prayed."

He pulled her by the arm.

Through the one eye hole, she saw a young, troubled face.

"Come on, Granny, move it."

Through the front room and into the yard he pulled her. "Get'n the car."

Moose cranked the engine.

Back on the Slope

George witnessed the scene and tried to run, but slipped.

The Sergeant caught him before he slid past.

A mournful cry escaped his lips. "Milll-llllie!"

The taxi roared away, up the opposite slope.

"Come on guys, back to the car. I don't know how they detected us, but we need to hurry."

Scrambling up the wet slope was even more difficult then coming down. It took ten minutes to cover the short distance. Jeremiah's crisp, white uniform was streaked with dirt everywhere. George's arms and bottom were muddy too.

The Sergeant lifted the mic. "This is car one. The kidnappers still have Ms. Butterfly. She is well enough to walk on her own, but they've fled the cove house and gone further west. All units, meet us at Brody's."

"Dad, you need to call Sam. Let them know that she's okay. I'll update my Chief Mate again."

"Hi Sam, how's Abby?"

She heard him in the background. "Is that George? Have they found Millie?"

"I'll put you on speaker, Abby is okay, stressed, but she's holding it together, go ahead George."

"We found where they were holding Millie, but somehow they realized we were close and pushed her into the car again and took off. At least she's not in the trunk this time."

Abigail's voice crackled over the speaker. "Not in the trunk, was she in the trunk before?"

"Yes, Abby, but she's okay and she's smart. She broke out their taillight from inside the trunk. That's how we tracked her. That woman is a wonder."

Her sympathetic voice soothed him. "George, dear, you must be suffering as much as I am. I'll try to be strong. I know you'll do everything you can to find my sister. I love you, George. You're a good man."

Tears filled his eyes. "Thank you, Abby, I love you too and I love Millie. I'll keep you informed. Sam, take care of Abigail."

"I will, George, be careful and bring our girl home."

"I won't come back, till I have her in my arms. Bye, Sam."

Jeremiah

Put me through to the Chief Mate. — Chief, we

located them, but somehow, they knew we were onto them and fled. — We're gathering at a local place to strategize. — Yeah, Brody's. I'll keep you informed." He hung up.

The Sergeant looked over at Jeremiah. "Captain, did he offer the name, Brody's?"

Jeremiah's eyes popped open wide. "Yes, he did. How did Lance know that?"

The Sergeant looked at the ground. "I have my suspicions. When my team arrives, I have a plan."

Only moments later three cars pulled up outside Brody's, two officers filed from each squad car.

"Team, this is the situation, I didn't want to put this on the radio, in case they are monitoring us. We have two men, holding Ms. Mildred Butterfly, she's alive, but in danger. The Captain has been regularly updating his Chief Mate, Lance, but we now suspect that his first officer is in league with the kidnappers, so this is what we're going to do." He glanced at Jeremiah. "I want the Captain to call his man again and tell him that we've used a drone with infrared technology to locate the kidnappers and that we're going to come in the backside, by Volcano Road. If our suspicions are correct, they will be flushed out onto this road. I want one car to go to Volcano Road, in case I'm wrong and I want one officer to set up on the ridge, just this side of Cove Road. When they pass that check point, he'll signal us and we'll throw out the stinger wire. That should stop them without flipping them. Car two, head to the back road. Car three, drop one officer at the ridge with a walkie, then bring the car back here to block the right side, just above Brody's Shack."

"Yes, Sarge." Two teams left.

"Team four, head to the Princess, but wait on the dock until we have them in custody and Ms. Butterfly is safely in our care."

He turned to Jeremiah. "Captain, I would like for you to ask your Head of Security to meet and assist members of team four. I would like to take your first officer into custody, because he's used my island to perpetrate his plan. Do you agree?"

Jeremiah rested his hands at his waist. "You have my full cooperation." He pulled his phone from inside his jacket and dialed. "Give me the Bridge. — We've used a drone with infrared technology to locate the kidnappers. We're going in the back way. We should be there in ten minutes. I'll let you know as soon as we have them."

He called the ship again. "Communications, connect me with the Head of Security. — Thank you." The line rang. "Chief, this is the Captain, I will be giving the order to send a local team aboard shortly. I want you and your two most trusted men to wait for them at the gangway and personally escort them. They'll give you instructions when they arrive. Do exactly as they say, no matter how crazy it sounds and tell no one of this order. Do you understand? — Good, I'll brief you when I arrive later." Jeremiah nodded to the Sergeant.

"It shouldn't be long now, if I'm correct about your first officer. I'm going to pull my car in with car three to block the road. Captain, I'd like for you and your father to wait at Brody's, would that be acceptable to you?"

Minutes ticked by.

They heard the Sergeant say, "They should have

been here by now, I don't understand."

The radio crackled.

George and Jeremiah heard the sound and dashed toward the patrol car.

"Uh, Sarge, this is car two, we've stopped the taxi and, you're not going to believe this, Ms. Butterfly is driving. What do you want us to do?"

"Is she okay?"

"Yes, sir."

"Please escort her to Brody's."

"Captain, Mr. Williams, I don't quite understand, but Ms. Butterfly will be here any minute."

The patrol car rolled up, followed by the taxi, now driven by a police officer.

George saw Mildred in the front seat and rushed to the door, before the vehicle had come to a complete stop and pulled it open.

"Millie, Millie, are you alright?"

"Yes, George, I'm fine, a little sore that's all."

He helped her out and wrapped his arms around her. "I don't want to hurt you, but I have to hug you."

She wrapped her arms around him as well.

The young kidnapper sat in the backseat of the taxi. The officer driving opened the rear door and ordered him out.

George and Jeremiah led Mildred to a bench outside of Brody's.

George knelt beside her. "Are you hungry, my love, or thirsty?"

"A little bit of both. I would love some water."

Jeremiah patted her on the shoulder. "Dad you stay with her, I'll get her something." But an officer handed Jeremiah a drink, he opened the bottle and handed Mildred the cold water, she tipped it up and drank half the bottle at one time, then brought it down. "Oh, my goodness, that's so good."

The Sergeant walked over. "Ms. Butterfly are you up to answering a few questions?"

"Yes, I believe I am."

Jeremiah walked to the food window and brought her a sandwich.

She took a big bite. "Oh, my goodness, this is amazing!" As she chewed, she said, "I thought you were going to have all your forces on Volcano Road—now, Sergeant, fire away."

Jeremiah sat down and offered his dad the seat next to her.

"First off, weren't there two kidnappers?"

"Yes, if one of your people would like to go collect, Moose, he's tied up back at the hut."

He nodded to two of his officers. They turned and headed back toward Volcano Road. "Now tell me about this young man who was in the car with you?"

"He was one of the kidnappers, but the Lord touched his heart and he helped me escape."

"Okay, we'll get the full story later, but for now do you know if they had an accomplice on the ship?"

"Yes, they did. They called him 'the boss.' I know he wore a white uniform. I heard his voice and it was familiar, but I couldn't remember where I'd heard it before."

The Sergeant waved. "Officer, bring the young man over here."

They walked up.

"Son, what's your name?"

The lad hung his head. "Robbie Ferguson, officer."

"Was there a man on the ship you called 'the boss'?"

"Yes, sir."

"Do you know his name?"

"I heard Moose call him Lance."

The Sergeant looked at Jeremiah, who nodded.

He hit the walkie, "Car four, execute the plan."

"Now Robbie, Ms. Butterfly said you helped her escape. Is that true?"

"Yes, sir."

"How did you get involved in a kidnapping in the first place?"

"My mom had lost her job and I met Moose. He said we could make some easy money. All we had to do was keep a nosey, old busybody away from the ship for a little while. Golly, I thought we'd show her around or something, then he made me put on a mask and he threw a hood over Ms. Millie's head …"

Jeremiah said, "Ms. Millie?"

"Yes, sir, that's what she told me to call her."

The Sergeant nodded. "Very well, the lady told you to call her Ms. Millie, so when did you know she was in real trouble?"

"When he punched her in the ribs, sir, but I was afraid of him too, so I kept quiet."

"What changed your mind, son?"

"Ms. Millie kept saying things about prayer and about God providing, it reminded me of my Granny Ferguson. The worse Moose got, the more I knew I'd want someone to help my Granny, if it were her, so when Ms. Millie told me she had an idea, I knew I should help her. She told me to tell Moose that she needed to go to the bathroom. She figured he'd let me take her outside, but instead, he gave me an old paint can and told me to tell her to use it. When she grabbed the can by the handle, she said, if David could use a stone on Goliath, she could use a half empty can of old, dried out paint on Moose. She told me to stand in the middle of the room and yell that she'd passed out. Now remember, her hands were still zipped-tied together," Robbie started to smile, "but when he came into the room, she jumped out from behind the door," he demonstrated, "she spun around like one of those big guys in the Highland Games who spin the rope with a big rock at the end. Well, she twirled around and conked him upside the head. He fell like Goliath! That's when I knew God was real."

Mildred smiled up at him. "And that's when he became my spiritual son. He repented and prayed with me right then and there to ask Jesus into his heart." She looked at the Sergeant. "And I hope you have no intention of arresting him."

"Well, Ms. Butterfly, the law is the law."

"And God's law trumps that." She stood up and placed her fists on her hips. "This boy is a new creation. You can't arrest him for what a different person did, now can you?"

"But …"

"Don't *but* me, officer." She turned toward Jeremiah. "And I believe you're short a couple of porters, aren't you?"

"But …"

"You don't *but* me either, Jeremiah. I now have two sons and I expect you to employ your brother."

His mouth hung open.

"Now unless you have something nice to say …"

Jeremiah cut his eyes toward the lad. "Robbie, would

you like a job as a porter on the Princess of the Sea?"

"I would love it, sir," he hung his head, "but I can't leave my mother all alone. She's crippled in one foot, she got hurt at work, you see and that's why she lost her job."

Mildred pulled her shoulders back. "I'm sure there is a job on the ship that a woman could do sitting down, isn't there, Jeremiah?"

He grinned from ear-to-ear. "Yes, ma'am, Millie."

She turned to the officer. "So, see, now you have one less criminal and two less unemployed people. Does that make you happy?"

George laughed. "You may as well give in." And he and Jeremiah laughed.

The mic clicked, "Sarge, this is car four, we have him."

"Good job, take him to the jail. Captain, would you like to accompany me?"

"Indeed, I would. Dad would you like for me to get someone to take you and Millie back to the ship?"

George looked at Millie. "Are you ready to go back?"

"Not yet, but let me call Abby, I know she's been so worried."

He pulled out his phone and handed it to her. "Just push redial."

Sam answered. "George?"

"No, it's Millie, is Abby there?"

On speaker phone, Abigail shouted, "Oh, Millie, are you okay?"

"I'm fine dear. We're going to take a couple of little detours before we come back to the ship. I'll see you for breakfast." She handed the phone back to George.

He asked, "A couple of detours?"

"Yes, we have to go tell Mrs. Ferguson the good news about her and Robbie's new jobs, then we'll go to the jail." She lifted her eyebrows and smiled. "Isn't that right, men?"

George held her hand tightly, smiled and nodded. "Whatever you decide, sweetheart."

While visiting Mrs. Ferguson, the sun began to rise.

Jeremiah said, "I'm sorry we're here so early, Mrs. Ferguson, but I find myself in quite a difficult spot. Would you be willing to start a new job today, I need, you and your son immediately, if you would like the jobs?"

Her smile filled the room more than the light edging in through the windows. "What type of work would we be doing?"

"Robbie will be a porter. Someone recently pointed out that I'm short a couple of hands." He smiled at Millie, then looked back at Mrs. Ferguson. "And as for you," he grinned, "we'll figure that out when we get there. What do you say?"

She threw her arms around the middle of his smudged uniform. "Maybe I could help with your laundry."

He laughed, "Yes, the last few hours have been quite an ordeal. I could definitely use some help. Now you and Robbie get some breakfast and pack. If you have any questions," he handed her a card, "call this number and ask for Shelly. Tell her I'm hiring you."

"Yes, sir, Captain."

As the door closed behind them and a shout went up. They all smiled.

At the jail, Chief Mate Lance sat in a cell.

Jeremiah, George and Millie approached.

Lance scowled through the bars.

Jeremiah stared at him. "Lance, I can't believe this. Why on earth would you betray me, betray your position, betray the ship and crew like this?"

"Well, Captain, with you and your little family-run business," he frowned at George. "I knew you'd keep hiring family members and that I'd gone as far as I was ever going to go with you, so I decided to take something for myself. Then when that old busybody," he tipped his chin toward Mildred, "got Ferdinand arrested, I figured out another way to get what was due me."

Jeremiah hung his head, then looked back through the bars. "You're right Lance, you'd gone as far as you were going to go with me," he pressed his lips together before continuing, "but our company is building a new ship called the Princess of the Med. She's to be a Mediterranean cruise liner and you were to be her Captain when she's finished in three months."

Lance dropped onto the bunk. "No way?"

"No way now, that's for sure." Jeremiah turned and

ushered his dad and Mildred through the door.

She patted his arm. "I'm so sorry Jeremiah."

Chapter 37

Back at the Ship

George accompanied Mildred to the infirmary. When they opened the door, the doctor was comforting Abigail with a hug.

Mildred laughed, causing Abigail to spin toward the familiar voice.

"Millie!" She rushed toward her. "Oh honey, I've been so worried."

She winked at Sam, "Yeah, I can see how you were suffering."

Abigail swatted her sister's hand, but grinned. "Oh, Millie, stop it."

Mildred laughed again and hugged her sister.

Sam insisted. "Mildred, we're so happy to have you

back safely! Please, come have a seat and let me examine you."

"I'm fine Sam. Just a few bumps and bruises. Besides, I can't let my sister's date check me over." She laughed.

"Nonsense!" He looked over his shoulder. "Nurse, come help Ms. Butterfly put on a gown."

Half an hour later, Sam came out to talk to Abigail and George. "She truly is a remarkable woman and she's okay. Like the lady said, only a few bumps and bruises. Luckily, that shot to her ribs didn't break any bones, but she's badly bruised."

Abigail gasped and put her hand over her mouth.

Sam smiled at her. "She will be sore for a couple of weeks, but she's okay, Abby."

From the other room they heard Mildred yell, "Can I put my clothes on now!"

They all laughed.

The doctor turned to Abigail. "Would you like to go help your sister? What she needs now is three weeks of rest."

Chapter 38

Last Full Day of the Cruise

Three romantic and restful weeks later, Abigail and Mildred sat on the foot of the cream-colored bedspread and Abigail clung to her sister's arm. "I can't believe how fast this past three weeks has gone by. Have you decided what you're going to do, Millie? You have to decide today, tomorrow morning, we arrive back home."

"You know, Abby, I was falling in love with George every time someone said that Mr. Cranky Pants had told them something or that our bills had been taken care of. I knew it had to be him somehow, but who knew Cranky Pants would be so handsome and part owner of this ship.

I mean, really! And I fell in love with his son, his granddaughters, and his grandson without even knowing their connections."

"So, what's the problem?"

She turned to Abigail with tear-filled eyes. "Do you think Max would approve?"

Abigail raised one finger to her chin. "Hmmm, let me see. Do you think Maxwell would want you to be happy?"

"Yes, I'm sure he would."

"Do you think Maxwell would approve of you having the children and grandchildren that the two of you could never have?"

"Yes, I know that he always lamented over the fact that we couldn't have children."

"Okay, do you think Maxwell would like George and his family?"

"But of course, he would, dear."

"Then what's the problem, Millie?"

She lowered her head and a tear rolled down her cheek. "Do you think Maxwell would think that I'm abandoning him?" Abigail put her arm around Mildred.

"No, dear, if Maxwell is where we think he is, he's wanting you to enjoy every moment of your life. Max loved you and he loved the Lord, just as George does. I think he would be appalled if you turned down a wonderful man who loves you."

Mildred wiped her face. "Thank you, Abby. That makes perfect sense, so," she wiped her face, "I've made up my mind. Yes, I'll marry George."

Abigail jumped up and clapped. "Yea! And do you want to make one more decision?"

With scrunched eyebrows, she turned her face toward Abigail. "What other decision do I need to make?"

She sat down again and grabbed Mildred's wrist. "You know how you've always loved …"

Chapter 39

That Night, the Last Night at Sea

The moon smiled down from the cloudless sky, the calm sea peeled past the bow of the ship as it sailed toward home, a light breeze refreshed the onlookers.

Captain Williams stood under a canopy of tiny sparkling lights, his back to the wind and he faced the superstructure of the ship.

Passengers lined both sides of the forward main deck.

George stood to his son's left, flanked by his grandson, Anthony.

A red carpet lined with soft white lights, lit the way for Shelly and Rebecca. They walked toward their dad, turned, then faced an open hatch. A beautiful orchestral arrangement of "Red Sails in the Sunset," played softly in the background.

Dr. Fielding exited the deck-level door, reached back and offered his hand to Abigail, who took it and stepped through. She wore a soft, sky-blue dress and carried a bouquet of white roses. He bent his left arm and she slipped her hand into his crooked elbow. He walked her down the aisle and toward the bridesmaids, then turned and stood beside her.

Everyone stared at the door again.

Robbie Ferguson stepped through the opening and offered his hand. Mildred followed, wearing the long, slinky white gown that they had once joked about saving for her next wedding. Her hair was styled in a glamorous twist with a soft flowing sweep in the front and she carried a bouquet of gorgeous, velvety blue, Ocean Breeze orchids. At her throat rested the sky-blue topaz necklace, no longer a loan from the ship, now a gift from her soon-to-be-husband.

The young man's bent arm, welcomed her hand, he walked her down the center carpet where George met her and they turned to face Jeremiah. The young man slipped into the crowd.

The Captain lifted a book and read. "Friends, family and shipmates, we are gathered here today before God, to join this man and this woman in holy matrimony. I am privileged to perform this ceremony between my father, George Williams and his beloved Mildred Van Camp Butterfly." A serious expression crossed his face, as he stared at the couple. "Now, in the sight of God and these witnesses, do you Mr. Cranky Pants take Ms. Grumpy Britches," but before he could complete the statement, people began to howl with laughter, he raised his voice over the roar, "to be your lawfully wedded wife?"

When the crowd quieted, George smiled at Mildred and said, "I most certainly do."

Chuckles continued.

"Do you Ms. Grumpy Britches take Mr. Cranky Pants to be your lawfully wedded husband?"

Mildred smiled at Jeremiah, then turned to look at George. "Indeed, I do, Captain Baby."

More raucous laughter broke out amongst the guests.

When the crowd quieted, Jeremiah quickly turned and said, "And do you, Doctor Samuel Fielding take," the statement sent shouts of joy and surprise through the crowd. Again, he raised his voice. "Ms. Abigail Van Camp Fine to be your lawfully wedded wife." Before the question was finished, applause spread through the crowd.

The two answered in turn, Sam first. "I do."

Then Abigail, "I do."

"By the powers vested in me, George and Mildred, I now pronounce you husband and wife," cheers and applause erupted, when they finally subsided, he turned to the other couple. "Samuel and Abigail, I now pronounce you husband and wife." Again, cheers burst forth. "Gentlemen, you may now kiss your brides."

As their lips met, the crowd cheered and whooped with joy.

Mildred leaned toward George's smiling face and whispered, "I always loved the double weddings at the end of Jane Austen's novels, didn't you, my love?"

The End!

THE FINE~BUTTERFLY DETECTIVE AGENCY

From the Author of the Kingdom Warriors
Christian Adventure Series
For ages 8 & up.

Book *1: The Sleeper Awakens*
Book *2: Cloud Skimmers*
Book *3: From the D.E.E.P.*
Book *4: Whisked Away* (upper teens)

Endnotes

i Thanks to our dear friend, Captain Kicker, for the Captain Baby anecdote.

ii Matthew 10:16.

iii Red Sails in the Sunset, first recorded by Lew Stone in England (1935-Joe Ferrie, vocal) and recorded many times since, by various artists.

iv My dear friend, Kay Wojack spurred me to add more romance. Thanks, Kay!

www.ingramcontent.com/pod-product-compliance
Lightning Source LLC
LaVergne TN
LVHW010312070526
838199LV00065B/5538